THE TUNER OF SILENCES

Biblioasis International Translation Series
General Editor: Stephen Henighan

Mia Couto

THE TUNER
OF SILENCES

TRANSLATED FROM THE PORTUGUESE
BY DAVID BROOKSHAW

BIBLIOASIS

Originally published as *Jesusalém*, Editorial Caminho, Lisbon,
Portugal, 2009.

FIRST EDITION

Library and Archives Canada Cataloguing in Publication

Couto, Mia, 1955-
        The tuner of silences / written by Mia Couto ; translated
by David Brookshaw.

(Biblioasis international translation series)
Translation of: Jesusalém.
ISBN 978-1-926845-95-1

        I. Brookshaw, David II. Title. III. Series: Biblioasis
international translation series

PQ9939.C68J4813 2012   869.3'42   C2012-901704-3

Edited by Stephen Henighan.

A work supported by the
Instituto Português do
Livro e da Biblioteca.

PRINTED AND BOUND IN USA

The entire history of the world is nothing more than a book of images that reflect the blindest and most violent of human desires: the desire to forget.

Herman Hesse, *Journey to the East*

CONTENTS

BOOK ONE

HUMANITY

I am the only man aboard my ship.
The rest are monsters devoid of speech,
Tigers and bears I lashed to the oars,
And my disdain reigns over the sea.

[…]
And there are moments when I nearly forget
A return of boundless delight.

My homeland is where the wind passes,
My beloved is where roses are in flower,
My desire the wing-print of birds,
I never wake from this dream nor ever sleep.

Sophia de Mello Breyner Andresen

I, MWANITO, THE
TUNER OF SILENCES

I listen, unaware
Whether what I hear is silence
Or god.
[...]

Sophia de Mello Breyner Andresen

I was eleven years old when I saw a woman for the first time, and I was seized by such sudden surprise that I burst into tears. I lived in a wasteland inhabited only by five men. My father had given the place a name. It was called, quite simply, Jezoosalem. It was the land where Jesus would uncrucify himself. And that was the end of the matter, full stop.

My old man, Silvestre Vitalício, explained to us that the world had come to an end and we were the only survivors. Beyond the horizon lay territory devoid of any life, that he referred to vaguely as "Over There." The entire planet could be summed up in a nutshell like this: stripped of people, with neither roads nor traces of any living creature. In those far-away places, even tormented souls had become extinct.

In Jezoosalem, on the other hand, there were only the living. Folk knew nothing of what it was like to yearn for the past or hope for the future, but they were alive. There we were, so alone that we didn't even suffer from any illnesses, and I believed we were immortal. Round about us, only animals and plants died. And when there was a drought, our nameless river faded into untruth, becoming a little stream that flowed around the back of our camp.

Mankind consisted of me, my father, my brother Ntunzi and Zachary Kalash, our servant who, as you will see, was not a man of any presence at all. And there was no one else. Or almost no one. To tell you the truth, I forgot two semi-inhabitants: the jenny, Jezebel, who was so human that she satisfied the sexual needs of my old father. And I also forgot my Uncle Aproximado. This member of the family needs special mention, for he didn't live with us in the camp. He lived next to the entrance gate to the game reserve, well beyond the permitted distance, and he only visited us from time to time. From where we lived to his hut was a farness full of hours and wild animals.

For us children, Aproximado's arrival was an excuse for great rejoicing, a jolt to our tedious routine. Uncle would bring us provisions, clothes, the basic necessities of life. My father would step out nervously to meet the truck piled high with our goods. He would intercept the visitor before he passed the fence that surrounded our dwellings. At this point, Aproximado was obliged to wash himself, so as not to bring in any contamination from the city. He would wash himself with earth and with water, no matter whether it was cold or whether night had fallen. After his bath, Silvestre would unload the truck, hurrying his delivery and hastening his departure. In a flash, quicker than a wing beat, Aproximado would once again disappear beyond the horizon before our anguished gaze.

—*He's not a real brother*— Silvestre would justify himself. —*I don't want too much talk, the man doesn't know our customs.*

This little cluster of humanity, joined like the five fingers on a hand, was, however, divided: my father, Uncle and Zachary were dark-skinned; Ntunzi and I were black as well, but had lighter skin.

—*Are we a different race?*— I asked one day.

My father replied: —*No one is from one race alone. Races*— he said —*are uniforms we put on.*

Maybe Silvestre was right. But I learnt too late that the uniform sometimes sticks to the soul of men.

—*You get that light skin from your mother, Dordalma. Little Alma had a touch of mulatto in her*— Uncle explained.

* * *

Family, school, other people, they all elect some spark of promise in us, some area in which we may shine. Some are born to sing, others to dance, others are born merely to be someone else. I was born to keep quiet. My only vocation is silence. It was my father who explained this to me: I have an inclination to remain speechless, a talent for perfecting silences. I've written that deliberately, silences in the plural. Yes, because there isn't one sole silence. Every silence contains music in a state of gestation.

When people saw me, quiet and withdrawn in my invisible sanctum, I wasn't being dumb. I was hard at it, busy in body and soul: I was weaving together the delicate threads out of which quiescence is made. I was a tuner of silences.

—*Come here, son, come and help me be quiet.*

At the end of the day, the old man would sit back in his chair on the veranda. It was like that every night: I would sit at his feet, gazing at the stars high up in the darkness. My father would close his eyes, his head swaying this way and that, as if his tranquillity were driven by some inner rhythm. Then, he would take a deep breath and say:

—*That was the prettiest silence I've ever heard. Thank you, Mwanito.*

It takes years of practice to remain duly silent. I had a natural gift for it, some ancestral legacy. Maybe I inherited it from my mother, Dona Dordalma, who could be sure? She was so silent, she had ceased to exist and no one even noticed that she no longer dwelt among us, the lively living.

—*You know son: there's the stillness of cemeteries. But the quiet of this veranda is different.*

My father. His voice was so discreet that it seemed just another type of silence. He coughed a bit and that hoarse cough of his was a hidden speech, without words or grammar.

In the window of the next house, the flickering light of an oil lamp could be seen. My brother was keeping an eye on us for sure. My heart was scuffed with guilt: I was the chosen one, the only one to share intimacies with our eternal progenitor.

—*Aren't we going to call Ntunzi?*

—*Leave your brother to himself. You're the one I like to be alone with.*

—*But I'm almost falling asleep, Father.*

—*Just stay a bit longer. I've got so much rage inside me, so much pent-up rage. I need to drown this rage, and I haven't got the strength.*

—*What rage is this, Father?*

—*For many years, I gave sustenance to wild beasts thinking they were household pets.*

I was the one who complained of feeling sleepy, but he was the one who was falling asleep. I left him nodding off in his chair and went back to the room where Ntunzi was waiting for me, wide awake. My brother looked at me with a mixture of envy and commiseration:

—*Did he give you all that nonsense about silence again?*

—*Don't talk like that, Ntunzi.*

—*That old man's gone mad. And to top it all off the guy doesn't like me.*

—*He does.*

—*Why doesn't he ever call me then?*

—*He says I'm a tuner of silences.*

—*And do you believe him? Can't you see it's all a big lie?*

—*I don't know, brother, what can I do if he wants me to sit there all nice and quiet?*

—*Don't you understand it's all just talk? The truth of it is you remind him of our dead mother.*

Ntunzi had reminded me a thousand times why my father had chosen me as his favourite. The reason for this preference of his had originated in one never-repeated instant: at our mother's funeral, Silvestre didn't know how to express his grief in public, and took himself off into a corner in order to cry his eyes out. That was when I approached my father and he got down on his knees so as to look into my three-year-old face. I raised my arms and instead of wiping away his tears, I placed my little hands over his ears. As if I were trying to turn him into an island and were distancing him from anything that had a voice. Silvestre shut his eyes inside this echoless haven: and he saw that Dordalma had not died. His arm stretched blindly in the shadow:

—*My dearest Alma!*

That was the last time he uttered her name. Nor did he ever again openly recall the time when he had been a husband. He wanted it all kept quiet, consigned to oblivion.

—*And you, my son, must help me.*

As far as Silvestre Vitalício was concerned, my vocation had been decided: I was to take care of this incurable absence, put out to pasture those demons that consumed his sleep. One time, when we were busy sharing our silence, I broached the subject:

—Ntunzi says I remind you of our mother. Is that so, Father?

—It's the opposite, you protect me from those memories. It's that Ntunzi who keeps bringing back the afflictions of the past to me.

—Do you know something, Father? Yesterday I dreamed of my mother.

—How can you dream of someone you never knew?

—I knew her, I just don't remember.

—That's the same thing.

—But I remember her voice.

—What voice? She hardly ever said a word.

—I can remember a peace that seemed, I don't know, that seemed like water. Sometimes I think I can remember the house, the great peacefulness of that house . . .

—And Ntunzi?

—What about Ntunzi, Father?

—Is he so sure he can remember your mother?

—Not a day goes by without him recalling her.

My father didn't answer. He brooded despondently for a while and then, his voice hoarse as if he'd been to the depths of his soul and back, he declared:

—I'm going to say this once and never again: you children can't remember anything or dream of anything at all.

—But I do dream, Father. And Ntunzi can remember so many things.

—It's all a lie. What you dream is what I produced in your heads. Do you understand?

—I understand, Father.

—And whatever you remember, I'm the one who planted it in your heads.

A dream is a conversation with the dead, a journey to the land of the souls. But there were no longer any dead, nor was there a territory for the souls. The world had ended and its demise brought with it obliteration: death without any dead. The

16

land of the departed had been annulled, the realm of the gods cancelled. That's what my father said all in one breath. Even today, I find Silvestre Vitalício's explanation harrowing and confusing. But at that particular moment, he was peremptory:

—*That's why you must neither dream nor remember. Because I don't dream or remember.*

—*But Father, don't you have any memory of our mother?*

—*Not of her, not of the house, not of anything. I don't remember anything any more.*

He got up with a groan to go and heat up the coffee. His steps were like a baobab pulling up its own roots. He looked at the fire as if he were looking at himself in a mirror, then closed his eyes and inhaled the aromatic steam rising from the coffee pot. And with his eyes still shut, he whispered:

—*I'm going to confess a sin: I stopped praying when you were born.*

—*Don't say that, Father.*

—*I'm telling you.*

Some people have children in order to get closer to God. He had become God when he became my father. That's what Silvestre Vitalício said. And he continued: the falsely downhearted, the insincere loners, they believe that their lamentations are heard in the heavens.

—*But God is deaf*— he said.

He paused so as to raise his cup and taste his coffee with relish, and then he insisted:

—*And even if he wasn't deaf: what is there to say to God?*

In Jezoosalem, there was no church of stone with a cross in it. My father made a cathedral out of my silence. It was there that he awaited God's return.

* * *

To be truthful, I wasn't born in Jezoosalem. I am, let us say, an emigrant from a place without name, geography, or history.

17

Straight after my mother died, when I was three, my father grabbed me and my elder brother and abandoned the city. He crossed forests, rivers and deserts until he reached what he guessed must be the most inaccessible spot. During our odyssey we passed thousands of people going in the opposite direction: fleeing the countryside for the city, escaping a rural war to seek shelter in an urban misery. People thought it strange: why was our family striking off into the interior, where the nation was burning?

My father was travelling up front, in the passenger seat. He looked sick, and perhaps thought he was travelling on a ship rather than in a road vehicle.

—*This is Noah's Ark on wheels*— he proclaimed as we were still taking our places in the old rattletrap.

Next to us, at the back of the truck, sat Zachary Kalash, the former soldier who helped my old man in his daily tasks.

—*But where are we going?*— my brother asked.

—*From now on there's no* where *to talk about*— Silvestre declared.

At the end of our great journey, we settled on a game reserve that had long been abandoned, and took shelter in an old camp that had once been used by hunters. Round about, all was emptiness because of the war, and there was no human presence whatsoever. Even animals were scarce. There was only an abundance of bushland, unpenetrated by any road for many years.

We settled in the ruins of the camp. My father in the central ruin, Ntunzi and I in a building next to it. Zachary made himself at home in an old shed out at the back. The old administrative building was left unoccupied.

—*That house*— my father said —*is inhabited by shadows and governed by memories.*

Later, he issued an order:

—*No one is to enter that place!*

Rebuilding work was minimal. Silvestre didn't want to disrespect what he called "the work of time." He did, however, busy himself with one task: at the entrance to the encampment, there was a little square with a pole, where flags were hoisted in the old days. My father turned the flagpole into a support for a huge crucifix. Above Christ's head, he fixed a sign which read: "Welcome, Mister God." This was his belief:

—*One day, God will come and apologize to us.*

Uncle and the old soldier Kalash crossed themselves frantically, so as to exorcize the heresy. We smiled confidently: we must be the beneficiaries of some divine protection as we never suffered an illness, or were bitten by a snake or pounced upon by a wild animal.

* * *

Time and time again, we would ask why we were there, so far away from everything and everyone. My father would reply:

—*The world has come to an end, my children. Jezoosalem is all that's left.*

I believed what my father said. But Ntunzi thought the whole story crazy. Embittered, he probed persistently:

—*So there's no one else in the world?*

Silvestre Vitalício took a deep breath, as if the answer required a great effort, and with a long, slow sigh, he murmured:

—*We are the only ones left.*

Vitalício was diligent, and devoted himself to our upbringing with great care and attention. But he made sure that his cares never gave way to tenderness. He was a man. And we were being schooled for manhood. We were the last and the only men. I remember that he would gently but firmly push me away when I tried to hug him:

—*Do you close yours eyes when you hug me?*

—*I'm not sure, Father, I'm not sure.*

—*You shouldn't do that.*

19

—Close my eyes, Father?

—No, hug me.

In spite of his physical reserve, Silvestre Vitalício always fulfilled the role of maternal father, an ancestor in the present. I found his devotion strange. For his zeal contradicted everything that he preached. His dedication would only make any sense if there were, in some undisclosed place, a time full of future.

—But, Father, tell us, how did the world die?

—To tell you the truth, I can't remember.

—But Uncle Aproximado . . .

—Uncle tells a lot of stories . . .

—Well then, you tell us, Father.

—It happened like this: the world finished even before the end of the world . . .

The universe had come to an end without a spectacle, with neither thunderclaps nor flashes of lightning. It had withered away, exhausted by despair. This was how my father prevaricated on the subject of the cosmos's extinction. First, the female places had begun to die: the springs, the beaches, the lagoons. Then, the male places had died: the towns, the roads, the ports.

—This was the only place left. This is where we've come to live for good.

To live? Surely, to live is to see dreams fulfilled, to look forward to receiving news. Silvestre didn't dream, nor was he waiting for news. In the beginning, all he wanted was a place where no one would recall his name. Now, he himself could no longer remember who he was.

Uncle Aproximado would douse the flames of these paternal musings. His brother-in-law had left the city for banal reasons common to those who felt overcome by age.

—Your father complained that he could feel himself growing old.

Old age isn't about one's years: it's fatigue. When we are old, everyone seems the same. That was Silvestre Vitalício's lamentation. People and places had become impossible to differentiate from each other when he undertook his final journey. Other times — and there were so many other times — Silvestre would declare: life is too precious to be squandered in a disenthralled world.

—*Your father is being very psychological*— Uncle concluded. — *He'll get over it one of these days.*

Days and years passed and father's ravings continued. In time, Uncle showed up less and less. As for me, his growing absences pained me, but my brother disabused me:

—*Uncle Aproximado isn't the person you think he is*— he warned me.

—*I don't understand.*

—*He's a jailer. That's what he is, a jailer.*

—*What do you mean by that?*

—*That dear little uncle of yours is the one who's guarding this prison we're being kept in.*

—*And why should we be in prison?*

—*Because of the crime.*

—*What crime, Ntunzi?*

—*The crime our father committed.*

—*Don't say such a thing, brother.*

All those tales our father invented about why we had abandoned the world, all those cock-and-bull stories had one purpose in mind: to befuddle us and remove us from our memories of the past.

—*There's only one truth: our old man is running away from the law.*

—*So what crime did he commit, then?*

—*One day I'll tell you.*

* * *

Whatever the reason for our exile, it was Aproximado who had led our retreat to Jezoosalem eight years before, driving us there in his rickety old truck. Uncle knew the place we were heading for. He had once worked on this reserve as a game warden. Uncle knew all about wild animals and guns, bush-lands and forests. While he drove us along in his old wreck, his arm dangling out of the window, he lectured us on the wiles of animals and the secrets of the bush.

That truck — the new Noah's Ark — reached its desti-nation, but breathed its last at the door of what would become our home. It was there that it rotted away, and there that it became my favourite toy, the refuge for my dreams. Sitting behind the wheel of the lifeless machine, I could have invented infinite journeys, conquered distances and obstacles. Like any other child, I could have travelled right round the planet until the whole world hung on my word. But this never happened: my dream had never learnt to travel. He who has always lived stuck in one place doesn't know how to dream of anywhere else.

With my capacity for illusion diminished, I eventually perfected other defences against nostalgia. In order to deceive the slowness of the hours, I would declare:

—*I'm off to the river!*

What usually happened was that no one heard me. Even so, I got so much pleasure from the announcement that I went on repeating it while I headed towards the valley. On the way there, I would pause in front of a lifeless telegraph pole that had been erected, but had never got as far as work-ing. All the other poles that had been stuck in the ground had turned into green shoots and were now trees with mag-nificent foliage. This particular pole was the only one stand-ing there like a skeleton, solitary in the face of infinity. That pole, according to Ntunzi, wasn't a post stuck in the ground: it was the mast of a ship that had lost its sea. That was why I always gave it a hug, as if seeking comfort from an old member of the family.

I would linger by the river in far-ranging reveries. I would wait for my brother who, at the end of the afternoon, would come down to bathe. Ntunzi would strip off his clothes and stand there, defenceless, gazing at the water with exactly the same look of yearning as when I saw him contemplating the suitcase that he packed and unpacked every day. Once, he asked me:

—*Have you ever been under the water, sonny boy?*

I shook my head, aware that I didn't understand the depth of his question.

—*Under the water*— Ntunzi said, —*you see things you'd just never imagine.*

I couldn't decipher my brother's words. But little by little, I got the idea: the most truly living thing in Jezoosalem was that nameless river. When it came down to it, the ban on tears and prayers had a purpose. My father wasn't as unhinged as we thought. If we had to pray or weep, it was to be right there, on the riverbank, upon bended knee on the wet sand.

—*Father always says the world has died, doesn't he?* Ntunzi asked.

—*But Father says so many things.*

—*It's the opposite, Mwanito. It's not the world that died. We're the ones who died.*

I shivered. I felt a chill pass through me, from my soul to my flesh, and from my flesh to my skin. So was death itself the place where we lived?

—*Don't say such a thing, Ntunzi. It scares me.*

—*Well, get this into your head: we didn't leave the world. We were pushed out, just like a thorn expelled by the body.*

His words pained me, as if life had skewered me, and in order to grow, I would have to prise its barb out of my body.

—One day, I'll tell you everything— Ntunzi drew the conversation to a close. *But for now, wouldn't my little brother like to take a look at the other side?*

—What other side?

—*You know, the other side: the world, Over There!*

I looked around me before answering. I was afraid our father might be watching us. I peeped up at the top of the hill, at the backs of the outbuildings. I feared Zachary might be passing by.

—*Go on, take your clothes off.*

—*You're not going to hurt me, are you, brother?*

I remembered he had once thrown me into the muddy waters of a pool and I'd got stuck, my feet tangled in the hidden roots of bulrushes.

—*Come with me*— he beckoned.

Ntunzi sank his feet in the mud and entered the river. He waded out until the water was up to his chest, and urged me to join him. I felt the current swirling around my body. Ntunzi gave me his hand, fearing I might be swept away by the waters.

—*Are we going to run away, brother?*— I asked, trying to contain my enthusiasm.

I couldn't understand why it had never occurred to me before: the river was an open highway, a channel that had been cleaved without let or hindrance. Our escape was right there and we hadn't been able to spot it. As my resolve grew stronger and stronger, I began to make plans out loud: who knows, maybe we should return to the riverbank and make a dugout? Yes, a little dugout would be enough for us to escape that prison and flow out into the wide world. I looked at Ntunzi, who remained impassive in the face of my daydreaming.

—*There'll be no dugout. Never. So forget it.*

Had I by any chance forgotten the crocodiles and hippos that infested the river further down? And the rapids and waterfalls, in a word, the countless dangers and traps that lay concealed in the river?

—*But has anyone been there? It's only what we've been told . . .*

—*Just calm down and be quiet.*

I followed him against the current and we waded our trail through the undulations until we reached a part where the river meandered ruefully, and the bed was carpeted with smooth pebbles. In this calm stretch, the waters were surprisingly clear. Ntunzi let go of my hand: I was to do as he did. Thereupon, he plunged in and then, while totally submerged, opened his eyes and looked up into the light as it reverberated off the surface of the water. I followed suit: from the river's womb, I contemplated the sparkling light of the sun. And its radiance fascinated me, enveloping me in a gentle daze. If there was such a thing as a mother's embrace, it must be something like this, this dizzying of the senses.

—*Did you like it?*

—*Did I hell? It's so beautiful, Ntunzi, they're like liquid stars, so bright!*

—*See, little brother? That's the other side for you.*

I dived in again, seeking to sate myself in that spirit of wonderment. But this time I had a fit of giddiness. I suddenly lost all notion of myself, confusing the depths with the surface. There I was, twisting around like a blind fish, unable to swim up to the surface. I would have ended up drowning if Ntunzi hadn't dragged me to the shore. Having recovered, I confessed that I had been seized by the chill of fear while underwater.

—*Could it be that someone is watching us from the other side?*

—*Yes, we're being watched. By those who will come and fish us.*

—*Did you say 'fetch us'?*

—*Fish us.*

I shuddered. The idea of our being fished, caught in the water, drew me to the horrifying conclusion that the others, those on the side of the sun, were the living, the only human creatures.

—*Brother, is it really true that we're dead?*

—*Only the living can know that, little brother. Only they.*

The accident in the river didn't inhibit me. On the contrary, I returned again and again to that bend in the river, and allowed myself to dive into the calm waters. And I would stay there endlessly, my eyes astonished, as I visited the other side of the world. My father never found out, but it was there, more than anywhere else, that I perfected my art as a tuner of silences.

MY FATHER, SILVESTRE
VITALÍCIO

[...]
You lived on the reverse
Endless traveller of the inverse
Free of your own self
Your own self's widower.

Sophia de Mello Breyner Andresen

I knew my father before I knew myself. That's why I've got a bit of him in me. Deprived of a mother's presence, Silvestre Vitalício's bony chest was my only source of comfort, his old shirt my handkerchief, his scrawny shoulder my pillow. A monotone snore was my only lullaby.

For years, my father was a gentle soul, his arms enveloped the earth, and the most time-honoured tranquillities nestled in their embrace. Even though he was such a strange and unpredictable creature, I saw old Silvestre as the only harbinger of truth, the sole foreteller of futures.

Now, I know: my father had lost his marbles. He noticed things that no one else acknowledged. These apparitions occurred mainly during the great winds that sweep across the savannah in September. For Silvestre, the wind was ghosts dancing. Windswept trees became people, the lamenting dead and trying to pull their own roots up. That's what Silvestre Vitalício said, shut away in his room and barricaded behind windows and doors, waiting for calmer weather.

—*The wind is full of sickness, the wind is just one big contagious disease.*

On those tempestuous days, the old man would not allow anyone to leave the room. He would call me to remain by his side, while I tried in vain to nourish silence. I was never able to calm him down. In the rustling of the leaves, Silvestre heard engines, trains, cities in movement. Everything that he tried so hard to forget was brought to him by the whistling of the wind in the branches.

—*But Father*— I ventured, —*why are you so scared?*

—*I'm a tree*— he explained.

A tree, yes, but without its natural roots. He was anchored in alien soil, in that fluid country he had invented for himself. His fear of apparitions worsened as time progressed. From trees, it spread to night's dark corners and to the earth's womb. At one stage, my father ordered the well to be covered over when the sun went down. Fearsome and malevolent creatures might emerge from such a gaping hole. This vision of monsters bursting from the ground filled me with fear.

—*But Father, what things can come out of the well?*

There were certain reptiles I didn't know about, that scratch around in tombs and bring back bits of Death itself under their nails and between their teeth. These lizards climb up the dank sides of wells, invade one's sleep and moisten the bed sheets of grown-ups.

—*That's why you can't sleep next to me.*

—*But I'm scared, Father. I just wanted you to let me sleep in your room.*

My brother never commented on my wish to sleep close to my father. In the dead of night, he would watch me creep furtively along the hall and stake out my place near the forbidden entrance to my father's quarters. Many times Ntunzi came and fetched me, lying like a rag on the floor and fast asleep.

—Come back to your bed. Father mustn't find you here.

I would follow him, too dazed to be grateful. Ntunzi would lead me back to bed and once, he even took my hand and said:

—Do you think you're scared? Well you may as well know that Father is much more scared.

—Father?

— Do you know why Father doesn't want you there in his room? Because he's scared to death that you'll catch him talking in his sleep.

—Talking about what?

— Inadmissible things.

Once again, it was Dona Dordalma, our absent mother, who was the cause of such strange behaviour. Instead of fading away into the distant past, she invaded the fissures of silence within night's recesses. And there was no way of putting the ghost to rest. Her mysterious death, without cause or visibility, had not stolen her from the world of the living.

—Father, has mother died?

—Four hundred times.

—What?

—I've told you, four hundred times: your mother died, every little bit of her, it's as if she was never alive.

—So where's she buried?

—She's buried everywhere, of course.

So maybe that was it: my father had emptied the world so as to be able to fill it with his inventions. At first, we were bewitched by the flighty birds that emerged from his speech and curled upwards like smoke.

—The world: do you want to know what it's like?

29

Our eyes answered by themselves. Yes of course, we yearned to know about it, as if the ground on which we stood depended on it.

—*Well, the world, children . . .*

And he would pause, his head swaying as if his ideas were being weighed, now this way, now that. Then, he would get to his feet, repeating with a cavernous voice:

—*The world, my children . . .*

In the beginning, I was afraid of these ruminations. Maybe my father just didn't know how to answer, and I found such weakness difficult to bear. Silvestre Vitalício knew everything and his absolute knowledge was the home that gave me protection. It was he who conferred names on things, it was he who baptized trees and snakes, it was he who foresaw winds and floods. My father was the only God we'd been given.

—*All right, you deserve to know, I'm going to tell you about the world . . .*

He began to sigh, and I began to sigh. Words had returned to him after all, and the light he cast brought me back once more to the firm ground of certainty.

—*Well it's all perfectly simple, children: the world has died, and all that's left is Jezoosalem.*

—*Don't you think there might be a woman survivor out there?*— My brother once suggested.

Silvestre raised an eyebrow. Ntunzi backed off, knowing his question was provocative: without women, we would have no seeds left. Father raised his arms and covered his head with them in an almost childlike response. Ntunzi repeated his theme, as if he were scraping a fingernail across glass.

—*Without women, there's no seed left . . .*

Silvestre's abruptness re-affirmed the old, but never openly stated prohibition: women were a forbidden subject, more so even than prayer, more sinful than tears or song.

—I won't have this talk. Women are forbidden to come here, and I don't even want to hear the word spoken . . .

—Calm down, Father, I just wanted to know . . .

—We don't talk about these things in Jezoosalem. Women are all . . . they're all whores.

We'd never heard him utter such a word. But it was as if a knot had been untied. From then on, for us, the term "whore" became another word to mean "woman." And on occasions when Aproximado forgot himself and launched forth on the subject of women, my old man would stumble through the house shouting:

—They're all whores!

For Ntunzi, such strange behaviour was proof of Silvestre Vitalício's growing insanity. As far as I was concerned, my father was suffering, at the most, from a passing illness. It was this infirmity that had us digging the rock-hard soil to make dry, lifeless wells, right in the middle of winter, precisely when the clouds were at their most barren.

At the end of the day, our father would inspect these skeletal pits, scratched out amid clods of earth and grit. To check the effectiveness of our toil, he would begin his inspection like this: A long rope was attached to Ntunzi's feet and he was lowered down into the rocky opening. We watched apprehensively, as he was gobbled up by the depths, barely connected to the world of the living. In Silvestre's hands, the taut rope was the opposite of an umbilical cord. My brother was hoisted back up to the surface, only for us to then go and open up another hole. We would end the day exhausted, covered in sand, our hair matted with dust. Occasionally, I would venture to ask:

—Why are we digging, Father?

—It's just for God to see. Just for Him to see.

God never did see, for where we were was too remote. Heavenly manna was never going to be poured into the burning pan of those holes. Silvestre wanted to render the Creator's work ugly, like that jealous husband who deformed his wife's face so that no one else could enjoy her beauty. His explanation, however, was completely different: the wells were nothing less than traps.

—*Traps? To catch which animals?*

—*They're other animals, ones that have come from afar. I can already hear them on the prowl near here.*

No matter how doubtful we were, we knew we wouldn't get any further explanations. A vague feeling that something inevitable was imminent came to dominate old Vitalício. The orders we began to get became more and more erratic. For example, under orders from Silvestre, I, my brother and Zachary Kalash began to sweep the footpaths. The verb "to sweep" was only correct in our father's language. For it was a kind of reverse sweeping: instead of clearing the paths, we spread dirt, twigs, stones and seeds over them. What, in fact, were we doing? In those nascent paths, we were killing any propensity they might have to grow and become roads. And in this way, we stifled any possible destination at birth.

—*Why are we wiping out the road, Father?*

—*I've never seen a road that wasn't sad*— he answered without taking his eyes from the wicker that he was plaiting to make a basket.

And as my brother wouldn't give up, so demonstrating his dissatisfaction with the answer, my father elaborated his argument. We could see very well what the road brought with it.

—*It brings Uncle Aproximado and our provisions.*

Silvestre pretended not to hear and continued impassively:

—*Waiting. That's what the road brings. And it's waiting that makes us grow old.*

So we went back to being imprisoned under barren clouds and aged skies. In spite of our solitude, we couldn't complain of having nothing to do. Our daily lives were regulated from sunrise to sunset.

The cycles of light and of the day were a serious matter in a world where the idea of a calendar had been lost. Every morning, our old man would inspect our eyes, peering closely into our pupils. He wanted to make sure we had witnessed the sunrise. This was the first duty of living creatures: to watch the creator's star emerge. By the light preserved in our eyes, Silvestre Vitalício knew when we were lying and when we had allowed ourselves too much time between the sheets.

—*That pupil's full of night.*

At the end of the day, we had other obligations that were equally inviolate. When we came to say good night, Silvestre would ask:

—*Have you hugged the earth, son?*

—*Yes, Father.*

—*Both arms open on the earth?*

—*A hug like the one Father taught us to give.*

—*Well, go to bed then.*

As a rule, he retired early, and didn't stay up after sunset. We would accompany him to his room and line up while he settled himself in his bed. Then, with a vague gesture, he would say in a husky voice:

—*You can go now. I've already started to leave my body.*

The next moment, he was asleep. That was when our home-made miracle would occur: candles would light up all by themselves in every corner of the house. Later, when I was already in bed, I would hear Ntunzi blowing firmly, ushering in the kingdom of the owls and of nightmares. From time to time, I would see my brother sleepwalking, exclaiming in a voice that wasn't his own:

—*Mateus Ventura, you're going to burn in the depths of hell!*

Even when he was asleep, my elder brother had to contest paternal authority. The name, Mateus Ventura, was one of the unmentionable secrets of Jezoosalem. In fact, Silvestre Vitalício had once had another name. Before, he had been called Ventura. When we moved to Jezoosalem, my father bestowed new names on us. Having been re-baptized, we were born anew. And we became even more deprived of a past.

The change in names was not a decision that was taken lightly. Silvestre prepared a ritual with due pomp and circumstance. As soon as the sun set, Zachary started to beat a drum and to recite, at the top of his voice, some impenetrable litany. Uncle, my brother and I gathered in the little square. There we stood, in silence, awaiting an explanation for why we had been summoned. That was when Silvestre Vitalício entered the square, wrapped in a sheet. He carried a piece of wood, and advanced towards the crucifix with the air of a prophet. He stuck the wood in the soil, and we could then see that it was a sign, upon which a name had been carved in bas-relief. Spreading his arms wide, my father proclaimed:

—*This is the last surviving country and it's going to be called Jezoosalem.*

Thereupon, he asked Zachary to bring him a can of water. He sprinkled a few drops on the ground, but then thought better of it. He didn't want to give the dead anything to drink. He scratched the earth with his foot until all vestiges had been erased. Having remedied his lapse, he announced in a solemn voice:

—*Let us now proceed to the de-baptism ceremony.*

And so we were each called forward in turn as follows: Orlando Macara (our dear Uncle Godmother) became Uncle Aproximado. My elder brother, Olindo Ventura, was transformed into Ntunzi. The assistant, Ernie Scrap, was renamed Zachary Kalash. And Mateus Ventura, my tormented progenitor, transformed himself into Silvestre Vitalício. I was the only one who kept the same name: Mwanito.

—*This one is still being born*— was how my father justified my keeping the same name.

I had various belly buttons, I had been born countless times, all of them in Jezoosalem, Silvestre revealed in a loud voice. And it would be in Jezoosalem that my final birth would be achieved. The world we had fled, the land of Over There, was so sad that one never wanted to be born.

—*I've never yet known anyone who was born for the pure joy of it. Maybe Zachary here . . .*

Kalash himself was the only one who laughed. And it was to be the selfsame Zachary who, by higher appointment, would officially register our new names.

—*Register the inhabitants in the population census, fill everything in on this piece of wood*— Father ordered, handing him an old hunting knife.

Zachary positioned himself hesitantly, sitting so that the wood was between his legs, and took a while to begin the register, twiddling the knife from finger to finger and from hand to hand:

—*Sorry, Vitalício. Is it register or rigester?*

—*Write down what I'm going to dictate.*

Zachary Kalash sculpted the letters with great care in bas-relief, as if each were a wound in a living body. Then, after a while, he stopped cutting:

—*Vitalício, with a small "v"?*

At this moment Uncle Aproximado interrupted the ceremony and asked Silvestre, if he was being serious, to at least honour his ancestors by naming his sons after them. It had always been like that, from generation to generation.

—*Placate our grandparents and give the boys their names. Protect the children.*

—*If there's no past, there are no ancestors.*

Aproximado left the ceremony, aggrieved. Ntunzi followed Uncle, leaving me without knowing what to do. The only one left was the soldier, sitting at my feet, and gazing up at the heavens in search of a solution to his orthographic uncertainties. Silvestre, full of pageantry, loosened the sheet round his neck and declared:

—*We are five people, but there are only four demons. You—* he pointed at me —*are missing a demon. That's why you don't need any name . . . for you, this is sufficient: boy, little lad, Mwanito.*

It was a moonlit night, and it was hard to get to sleep. My father's recent words on my incomplete birth echoed within me. And it occurred to me that I was to blame for my own orphanhood. My mother had died not because she had ceased to live, but because she had separated her body from mine. Every birth is an exclusion, a mutilation. If I had my way, I'd still be part of her body, and we would be bathed by the same blood. They talk of "parturition." Well, it would be more correct to talk of "departurition." I wanted to make amends for my departure.

* * *

The war robbed us of memories and hopes. But strangely enough it was the war that taught me to read words. Let me explain: the first letters I learnt were the ones I deciphered on the labels that were stuck on the crates of weapons. Zachary Kalash's room, at the rear of the camp, was a real arsenal. The "Minister of War" was what Father called him. When we arrived at Jezoosalem, arms and munitions were already stored there. Zachary chose to install himself among them. And it was in that very hut that the soldier surprised me deciphering the labels on the containers.

—*That's not for reading, laddie—* the old soldier scolded me.

—*Not for reading? But they look like letters . . .*

—*They look like them, but they're not. That's Russian, and not even Russians know how to read the Russian language . . .*

Zachary hastily tore up the labels. Then, he handed me some others that he took from a drawer, and that he said were the translation of the Russian originals, done by the Ministry of Defence.

—*You just read these papers that are in pure Portuguese.*

—*Teach me to read, Zaca.*

—*If you want to learn, then learn by yourself.*

Learn by myself? Impossible. But more impossible still was to hope that Zachary might teach me anything at all. He knew my father's orders. In Jezoosalem, no books were admitted, or notebooks, or anything at all associated with writing.

—*Well then, I'll teach you to read.*

That's what Ntunzi said later. I declined. It was too risky. My brother had already shown me how to see the other side of the world in the river. I didn't want to think about how old Silvestre would react if he came to know of his first-born's transgressions.

—*I'll teach you to read*— he repeated emphatically.

So that was how I began my first lessons. Some learn with spelling books, in classrooms. I began by spelling out the weapons of war. My first school was an ammunition dump. Classes were held in the semi-darkness of a storage shed, during the long periods when Zachary was out, shooting in the bush.

I was already putting words together, weaving sentences and paragraphs. I very quickly realized that, instead of reading, I had a tendency to intone, as if I were in front of a musical score. I didn't read, but sang, thus magnifying my disobedience.

—*Aren't you scared we'll get caught, Ntunzi?*

—*You should be scared of not knowing anything. After reading, I'm going to teach you how to write.*

It wasn't long before we began clandestine writing lessons. Scribbling in the sand of the yard with a little piece of kindling wood, I was fascinated, and felt the world being reborn, like the savannah after the rains. I gradually came to understand Silvestre's prohibitions: writing was a bridge between past and future times, times that had never existed in me.

—*Is this my name?*

—*Yes. M-w-a-n-i-t-o, that's what's written. Can't you read it?*

I never told Ntunzi, but at the time, I had the impression that I wasn't learning with him. My real teacher was Dordalma. The more I deciphered the words, the more my mother, in my dreams, gained physical and vocal expression. The river made me see the other side of the world. Writing returned my mother's lost face to me.

On Aproximado's next visit, Ntunzi stole the pencil he used to note down our orders for provisions. My brother solemnly twirled the pencil with the tips of his fingers and told me:

—*Hide it well. This is your weapon.*

—*So where shall I write? Do I write on the ground?*— I asked, in a whisper.

Ntunzi replied that he'd already given the matter some thought. And he walked off. Not long after, he reappeared with a pack of cards.

—*This will be your school notebook. If the old man appears, we'll pretend we're having a game.*

—*Write on a pack of cards?*

—*What other paper is there round here?*

—*But with the pack we use to play?*

—*Precisely for that reason: Father will never suspect. We already cheat at cards. Now, we'll cheat at life.*

So that's how I began my first diary. It was also how aces, jacks, queens, kings, deuces and the seven of hearts began to share my secrets. My minute scrawl filled hearts, clubs, diamonds and spades. Into those fifty-two little squares of paper, I poured a childhood of vexations, hopes and confessions. In my games with Ntunzi, I was always the loser. But I lost myself in my games with writing.

Every night, after my jottings, I would wrap the pack of cards up and bury it in the back yard. I would return to my room and gaze enviously at Ntunzi's face as he slept. I had already learnt to glimpse the liquid lights of the river, and I already knew how to travel across written letters as if each one were an endless highway. But I still needed to know how to dream and to remember: I wanted that boat that took Ntunzi to the arms of our dead mother. On one occasion, my anger overflowed:

—*Father says it's a lie, he says you don't dream about our mother.*

Ntunzi looked at me with pity, as if I were disabled and that my organ for dreaming had been damaged.

—*Do you want to dream? You're going to have to pray, little brother.*

—*Pray? Don't you know that Father . . .*

—*Forget Father. And I said it's if you want to dream.*

—*But I've never prayed. I don't even know how it's done . . .*

—*Give me one of the cards, and I'll write a prayer on it for you to learn by heart. Then, you'll start dreaming, just you see.*

I dug up the pack and handed him an ace of diamonds. He would have space enough around the red lozenge to scribble the sacred words.

—*No, not that one. You'd better give me a queen. It's because it's a prayer to Our Lady.*

I guarded that card as if it were the most precious thing I would ever possess in my life. When I knelt down by my bed, my heart would stumble over that little prayer. Until, one day, the soldier Zachary surprised me as I was mouthing the litany.

—*Are you singing, Mwanito?*

—*No, Zaca, it's nothing. It's Russian. I learnt the labels that were left.*

39

I didn't have a leg to stand on with my lie. Zachary, of course, was spying on us under orders from Silvestre. We were immediately summoned before him. My father already had his charges prepared against Ntunzi:

—*It was you who taught your little brother.*

Foreseeing violence, I rushed forward to defend my brother:

—*I learnt it without Ntunzi knowing.*

—*No one prays here!*

—*But Father, what's so bad about it?*— Ntunzi asked.

—*To pray is to summon visitors.*

—*But what visitors, if there's no one else in the world?*

—*There's Uncle . . .*— I improvised a correction.

—*Shut up, who told you to talk?*— my brother shouted.

Old Silvestre smiled, pleased at his elder son's desperate behaviour. He didn't have to intervene, his son was receiving his punishment in another way. Ntunzi noted his father's satisfaction and took a deep breath in order to control himself. His tone was more measured by the time he spoke again:

—*What visitors from outside could we have? Explain it to us, Father.*

—*There are visitors we can have without even being aware of it. They're angels and demons who turn up without so much as a by your leave . . .*

—*Angels or demons?*

—*Angels or demons, there's no difference between them. The difference lies in us.*

Silvestre's raised arm left no room for doubt: the conversation had exceeded its limits. It was made clear that there was to be no more praying, ever. And that was it, period, there was only one resolution and that was irrefutable.

—*And you!*— my father proclaimed, pointing at me: —*I don't want to hear you crying ever again.*

—*When did I ever cry, Father?*

—Just now, you were snivelling.

And just as he was leaving, Ntunzi showed that he wanted to have the last word. Before Silvestre's astonished gaze, he asked:

—No praying or crying?

—Crying or praying, it's all the same thing.

* * *

The following night, I was woken by the roar of lions. They were nearby, maybe they were even prowling round the corral. In the darkness of the room, I hugged myself to try and get to sleep. Ntunzi was dead to the world while I was unable to curb my fear, and went to find shelter under my father's bed. In that clandestine intimacy, flat out on the cold floor, I was lulled to sleep by his snores. But not long afterwards, I was discovered and expelled angrily.

—Father, please, let me sleep with you just this once.

—People sleep together in the cemetery.

I returned to my bed, unprotected, and listened to the roars of the big cats, which came ever nearer. At that moment, as I stumbled around defenceless in the dark, I hated my father for the first time. As I settled down in bed, my heart was seething with fury.

—Shall we kill him?

Ntunzi was leaning on his elbow in bed, waiting for my answer. He waited in vain. My voice had stuck in my throat. He pressed on:

—The bastard killed our mother.

I shook my head, desperately refuting the idea. I didn't want to listen. I wished I could hear the lions roaring again so that they might block out my brother's voice.

—Don't you believe it?

—No— I murmured.

—Don't you trust me?

41

—Maybe.

—Maybe?

That "maybe" was an added burden on my conscience. How could I admit the possibility that my father might be a murderer? For a long time I tried to assuage this guilt. And I mulled over possible underlying reasons: if something had happened, my father must have acted against his will. Who knows, perhaps he had done so in illegitimate defence? Or maybe he had killed out of love and, in carrying out the crime, half of him had died as well?

The truth is that, as an absolutist ruler over his own solitude, my father was losing his wits, a refugee from the world and from the rest of humanity, but unable to escape from himself. Perhaps it was this despair that made him surrender to a personal religion, a very special interpretation of the sacred. Generally speaking, the role of God is to forgive us our sins. For Silvestre, God's existence allowed us to hold Him responsible for the sins of humanity. In this reverse version of faith, there were no prayers or rituals: a simple cross at the entrance to the camp guided God on his arrival at our reserve. And there was a welcome sign above the cross, which read: "Welcome, illustrious visitor!"

—That's so that God knows we've forgiven him.

This hope of a divine apparition provoked a scornful smile from my brother:

—God? We're so far from anywhere, that God would get lost on the way here.

* * *

On our way to the river the following morning, we were not accosted by celestial creatures, but by my father, spitting anger. He was with Zachary Kalash, who kept himself out of it while Silvestre was getting ready to be taken over by violence.

—*I know what you're up to down by the river. The two of you, all naked . . .*

—*We're not doing anything, Father*— I hastened to answer, puzzled by his insinuation.

—*Keep out of this, Mwanito. Go back home with Zaca.*

Over and above my own sobbing, I could hear the blows Silvestre was directing against his own son. Kalash even made a move to go back. But he ended up pushing me into the darkness of my room. That night, Ntunzi slept lashed to the fence. Next morning, he was ill, shivering with fever. It was Zachary who walked through the mist and carried him back to the room, while our dear Ntunzi was being brushed by death. It was barely light when I heard Silvestre, Zachary and Uncle Aproximado their footsteps whirling around the room. As morning progressed, I could no longer pretend I was asleep. Ntunzi, my only brother, only companion of my childhood, was slipping away towards the beyond. I left my room and armed with a stick, I began to write in the sand all around the house. I wrote and wrote, feverishly, as if I were set on occupying the entire landscape with my scribbling. The ground round about gradually became a page upon which I sowed my hope for a miracle. It was a supplication to God to hasten his arrival in Jezoosalem and save my poor brother. Exhausted, I fell asleep, prostrate over my own writing.

It was already day when Zachary Kalash shook me from my sleep, and tugged at my elbow:

—*Your brother is burning. Help me take him down to the river.*

—*I'm sorry, Zachary, but wouldn't it be better for Father to do that?*

—*Keep quiet, Mwanito, I know what I'm doing.*

The river was the last hope of a cure. The soldier and I transported Ntunzi in a little handcart. His swaying legs looked as if they were already dead. Zachary immersed my poor brother's lifeless body in the waters, plunging him in and out of the current seven times. But Ntunzi didn't show any improvement, nor did the fever cease burning his scrawny body.

Faced with the likely outcome, Uncle Aproximado wanted to take the boy to a hospital in the city.

—*I beg you, Silvestre. Go back to the city.*

—*What city? There is no city.*

—*Put an end to this. This madness can't go on any longer.*

—*There's nothing to put an end to.*

—*You know the pain of losing your wife. Well, you'd never get over the death of a son.*

—*Leave me alone.*

—*If he dies you'll never be left alone. You'll be haunted by your second tormented spirit . . .*

Silvestre only just managed to restrain himself. His brother-in-law had gone too far. My father gripped the arms of his chair so hard that it was as if the opposite were the case and the wood were securing him to the seat. Gradually his chest relaxed, and he gave a deep, long sigh:

—*Well now, let me ask you this, my dear Orlando, or rather, my dear Brother-in-law: did you wash yourself when you reached the entrance to Jezoosalem?*

—*I won't even bother to answer.*

—*So it was you who brought Ntunzi's illness with you.*

He picked Uncle up by the scruff of his neck and shook him around in his clothes like a rattle. Did he know how and why the family had escaped wild animals, snakes, illnesses and accidents up until then? It was simple: in Jezoosalem, there were no dead, no one risked encountering graves, the weeping of the bereaved, or the wailing of orphans. Here, there was no yearning for anything. In Jezoosalem, life didn't owe anyone an apology. And at that moment, he felt no obligation to provide any more explanations.

44

—*So you can go back to your stinking city. Get out of here.*

* * *

Aproximado still slept with us that night. Before he fell asleep, I went over to his bed, determined to confess something to him:

—*Uncle, I think it's my fault.*

—*What's your fault?*

—*I was the one who made dear Ntunzi fall ill.*

This was why: I'd gone along with his wish that we should kill our old man. Aproximado rested his big round hand on my head, and smiled kindly:

—*I'm going to tell you a story.*

And he spoke of some father or other who didn't know how to give his son enough love. One night, the hovel in which they lived caught fire. The man picked the child up in his arms and left the scene of the tragedy, trudging through the night. He must have crossed the borders of this world, for when he eventually put the child down on the ground, he noticed that there was no more earth. All that remained was emptiness upon emptiness, shredded clouds among faded skies. The man concluded to himself:

—*Well now, my son will only ever find ground on my lap.*

That little boy never realized that the vast territory where he later lived, grew up and made children, was no more than his old father's lap. Many years later, when he opened up his father's grave, he called his son and said to him:

—*Do you see the soil, son? It looks like sand, stones and clumps of earth. But it's arms as well, and its arms will embrace you.*

I patted Uncle's hand, and returned to my bed, where I lay wide awake for the rest of the night. I was listening to Ntunzi's heavy breathing. And it was then that I noticed he was coming back to life. Suddenly, his hands stretched out feeling the darkness, as if he were looking for something. Then he moaned, almost on cue:

—*Water!*

I rushed over, holding back my emotions. Aproximado woke up and switched on a torch. The focus of its light veered away from us and meandered down the hall. The next moment, the three adults came into the room and hurried over to Ntunzi's bed. Silvestre's trembling hand sought out his son's face and he saw that he was no longer feverish.

—*The river saved him*— Zachary exclaimed.

The soldier sank to his knees next to the bed and took Ntunzi's hand. The other two adults, Aproximado and Silvestre, stood there facing each other, silent. Suddenly, they hugged each other. The torch fell to the ground and only their legs were visible, tottering nervously backwards and forwards. They were like two blind men in a clumsy dance. For the first time, Silvestre treated his brother-in-law with fraternal affection:

—*I'm sorry, brother.*

—*If that nephew of mine had died, you'd have nowhere else in the world to hide . . .*

—*You know very well how much I care for these kids. My sons are my last hope in life.*

—*But you're not helping them like this.*

You don't help a bird to fly by holding onto its wings. A bird flies when it's quite simply allowed to be a bird. That's what Uncle Aproximado said. Then he left, engulfed by the darkness.

MY BROTHER, NTUNZI

Do not seek me there
where the living visit
the so-called dead.
Seek me in the great waters.
In the open spaces,
in a fire's heart,
among horses, hounds,
in the rice fields, in the gushing stream,
or among the birds
or mirrored in some other being,
climbing an uneven path.

Stones, seeds, salt, life's stages.
Seek me there.
Alive.

Hilda Hilst

M y brother Ntunzi had only one aspiration in his life: to escape from Jezoosalem. He had known the world, had lived in the city, and remembered our mother. I envied him for all this. Countless times I begged him to tell me about this universe that was unknown to me, and each time, he would linger on details, the colours and the bright lights. His eyes shone, swollen with dreams. Ntunzi was my cinema.

Incredible though this may seem, the person who had stimulated him in the art of telling stories had been our father. Silvestre thought that a good story was a more powerful weapon than a gun or a knife. But that had been before our arrival at Jezoosalem. At that time, and in the face of complaints about conflicts at school, Silvestre had encouraged Ntunzi: "If they threaten you with a beating, answer with a story."

—*Is that what Father said?*— I asked, surprised.

—*That's what he said.*

—*And did it work?*— I asked.

—*I got beaten up all the time.*

He smiled. But it was a sad smile because, in truth, what story was there to invent now? What story can be conceived without a tear, without song, without a book or a prayer? My brother's expression became gloomy, and he grew old before my very eyes. On one occasion, his sorrow was expressed in a strange way:

—*In this world there are the living and the dead. And then there's us, the ones who have no journey to make.*

Ntunzi suffered because he could remember, he had something to compare this with. For me, our reclusion was less painful: I had never experienced any other way of living.

I would sometimes ask him about our mother. That was his cue. Ntunzi would blaze like a fire fuelled by dry wood. And he would put on a complete performance, imitating Dordalma's manner and voice, each time adding in one or two new revelations.

On the occasions when I forgot or neglected to ask him to revisit these memories, he would soon react:

—*So aren't you going to ask me about Mama?*

And once again, he would re-kindle his memories. At

the end of his performance, Ntunzi would become subdued again, just as happens with drunks and their euphoria. Knowing that the outcome would be sad, I would interrupt his theatre to ask:

—And what about the others, brother? What are other women like?

Then, his eyes would gleam anew. And he would turn on his heels, as if exiting an imaginary stage before re-emerging from the wings to imitate the ways of women. He would bunch his shirt up to simulate the bulk of a woman's bosom, wiggle his buttocks and reel around the room like a headless chicken. And we would collapse on the bed, dying of laughter.

Once, Ntunzi told me of some old crush he'd had, a product more of his delirium than of lived experience. Not that it could have been otherwise: he had left the city when he was only eleven years old. Ntunzi dreamed his women with such ardour that they became more real than if they were flesh and blood. On one occasion, when he was in the middle of his hallucinations, he met a woman of boundless beauty.

When the apparition touched his arm and he looked at her, a cold shiver ran through him: the girl had no eyes. Instead of sockets, what he saw were two empty holes, two bottomless wells without sides.

—What's happened to your eyes?— he asked unsteadily.

—What's wrong with my eyes?

—Well, I can't see them.

She smiled, astonished at his awkwardness. He must be nervous, unable to see properly.

—You can never see the eyes of the one you love.

—I understand— Ntunzi affirmed, recoiling with all due care.

—Are you scared of me, my little Ntunzi?

One more step backwards and Ntunzi lost his footing, tumbling into an abyss, and he is still falling, falling, falling, even today. As far as my brother was concerned, the lesson was clear. People who allow passion to take them by storm are destined to become blind: we stop seeing those whom we love. Instead, a lovesick man stares into his own abyss.

—*Women are like islands: always distant, but quelling all the sea around them.*

For me, all this was like thickening swirls of mist that merely made the mystery surrounding Woman more dense. I spent whole afternoons gazing at the queens on the playing cards, and thinking to myself that if those were true reproductions, then Ntunzi's ravings had no basis whatsoever. They were as masculine and as arid as Zachary Kalash.

—*Women sometimes bleed*— my brother once told me.

I was baffled by this. Bleed? We all bleed; why did Ntunzi invoke that particular attribute?

—*A woman doesn't need to get injured, she's born with a gash inside her.*

When I addressed this question to Silvestre Vitalício, he answered: women were injured by God. And he added: she got slashed when God chose to be a man.

—*Did my mother bleed too?*

—*No, not your mother.*

—*Not even when she died?*

—*Not even then.*

The vision of a stream of blood flowing out of Silvestre's body disturbed my dreams that night. It rained blood and the river was growing red, and my brother was drowning in the flood it caused.

And I dived into the waters to try and rescue his body, which was tiny and fragile, like that of a newborn baby, and fitted in my arms. Silvestre's slurred speech echoed deep within me:

—*I'm a male, but I bleed like women.*

* * *

One time, my father came into our room and caught my brother doing one of his acts, busy imitating what he called a "showy woman." Silvestre's eyes grew red as if injected with hatred:

—*Hey, who are you imitating? Who is it?*

Whereupon he hit him so hard that my poor brother lost consciousness. I placed myself between them, offering up my body to placate our father's fury, and I shouted:

—*Father, don't do this, my brother has almost died so many times!*

And it was true: after having burned with fever, my brother continued to suffer from attacks. Ntunzi would swell up like a ball, his eyes dazed, his legs rubbery like some punch-drunk dancer. Then, all of a sudden, he would collapse on the floor. When this happened, I would hurry away for help, and Silvestre Vitalício would saunter over, repeating to himself words that were either a curse or a diagnosis:

—*A burn on the soul!*

Our old father had an explanation for these relapses: too much soul. An illness picked up in the city, he concluded. And raising his finger, he would growl:

—*That's where your brother caught this scourge. It was there, in that infernal city.*

His therapy was simple but effective. Every time Ntunzi suffered these convulsions, my father would kneel on his chest and, using his fingers like a knife blade, he would apply increasing pressure on his throat. It looked as if he was going to asphyxiate him but, suddenly, my brother would deflate like a pricked balloon, and the air flowing between his lips produced a noise that was a bit like the braying of our jenny, Jezebel. When Ntunzi was empty, my father would lean right

51

over until he was almost brushing his face and solemnly whisper:

—*This is the breath of Life.*

He would take a deep breath and blow strongly into Ntunzi's mouth. And when his son began to jerk, he concluded triumphantly:

—*There! I've given birth to you.*

We should never forget, he stressed. And he repeated, breathless, his eyes defiant:

—*Your mother may have pulled you from the darkness. But I have given birth to you many more times than she did.*

He withdrew from our room in triumph. Not long afterwards, Ntunzi recovered his sanity and passed his hands right down his legs as if to make sure they were still intact. And that's how he remained, with his back to me, regaining his existence. On one such occasion, I noticed his back shuddering with sadness. Ntunzi was weeping.

—*What's wrong, brother?*

—*It's all a lie.*

—*What's a lie?*

—*I don't remember.*

—*You don't remember?*

—*I don't remember Mama. I can't remember her . . .*

Every time he had acted out her part in such lively fashion, it had been pure pretence. The dead don't die when they stop living, but when we consign them to oblivion. Dordalma had perished once and for all and, for Ntunzi, the time of his early childhood when the world had been born along with him had been extinguished forever.

—*Now, my little brother, now we really are orphans.*

Maybe Ntunzi felt his orphanhood from that night on. But for me, the sentiment was more bearable: I had never had a mother. I was merely the son of Silvestre Vitalício. For that reason, I couldn't surrender to the invitations my

brother directed towards me on a daily basis: that I
should hate our father. And that I should wish him dead
as strongly as he did.

* * *

Whether because of his illness or his despair, Ntunzi's behaviour changed. Without the false nourishment of his memories,
he became embittered, full of gall. His nights began to be
taken up with a certain ritual: he would painstakingly pack the
few possessions he had in an old suitcase, which he then hid
behind the wardrobe:

—*Never let Father see this.*

First thing in the morning, with the same case resting on
his feet, Ntunzi would sit engrossed in an ancient map that
Uncle Aproximado had once given him in secret. With his
index finger, he roamed again and again over the print, like a
canoe drifting drunkenly down imaginary rivers. Then, he
would scrupulously fold the map again and place it in the bottom of the suitcase.

On one occasion, while he was locking it, I ventured:

—*Brother?*

—*Don't say anything.*

—*Do you want some help?*

—*Help for what?*

—*Well, to put your case away . . .*

Perching on the chair, we pushed the case onto the top of
the cupboard while Ntunzi murmured to himself:

—*You old son-of-a-bitch, you murderer!*

* * *

Some nights later, Ntunzi fell asleep, lulled by reading his
map. The prohibited guide to journeys slipped and came to
rest next to his pillow. That's where my father found it the following morning. Silvestre's fury made us jump from our beds:

53

—Where did you get this filth?

Silvestre didn't wait for an answer. He tore up the old map, and then ripped it again into ever smaller pieces, on and on, until it seemed as if he was going to shred his own fingers. Cities, mountain ranges, lakes, roads, all fluttered to the floor. The entire planet was dissolving on the floor of my room.

Ntunzi stood there gaping, rooted to the spot, as if his very soul were being hacked to pieces. I took a deep breath and mumbled incomprehensibly. But Father was already leaving, and yelled:

—No one touch anything! Zachary is the one who'll come and clean up this shit.

Shortly afterwards, the soldier burst into the room, carrying a broom. But he didn't sweep up. He picked up the little pieces one by one, and threw them up in the air like a witch-doctor casting cowrie shells. The paper flurried and scattered across the floor in whimsical designs. Zachary read these shapes and, after a little while, called me over to him:

—Come, Mwanito, come and see . . .

The soldier was sitting in the midst of a constellation of little bits of coloured paper. I went over while he pointed, his finger shaking:

—See here, this is our visitor.

—I can't see anything. What visitor?

—The one who's on her way.

—I don't understand, Zaca.

—Our peace is coming to an end, here in Jezoosalem.

* * *

Next morning, Ntunzi awoke, his mind made up: he was going to run away, even if there was no other place. Our father's latest aggression had led him to this decision.

—I'm leaving. I'm getting out of here, for good.

The case clutched in his hand reinforced the strength of his intention. I ran and seized his hands, begging him:

—*Take me with you, Ntunzi.*

—*You're staying.*

And off he went down the track, with a nimble stride. I went after him, crying inconsolably, repeating amid my snivelling and my sobs:

—*I'm going with you.*

—*You're staying. I'll come back for you later.*

—*Don't leave me on my own, please, dear brother.*

—*I've made up my mind.*

We walked for hours, ignoring all perils. When we eventually arrived at the entrance to the reserve, my heart felt overloaded. I shuddered, terrified. We'd never ventured so far. This was where Uncle Aproximado's hut was. We went in: it was empty. As far as we could see, no one had lived there for a long time. I still wanted to take a closer look at the place, but Ntunzi was in a hurry. Freedom was there, just a few yards away, and he ran to open the wooden doors.

When the big old doors were fully open, we saw that the much heralded road was no more than a narrow track that was almost indiscernible, overgrown with elephant grass and invaded by termite hills. But as far as Ntunzi was concerned, the little path was an avenue that crossed the very centre of the universe. That narrow little footpath was enough to fuel his illusion that there was another side to the world.

—*At last!*— Ntunzi sighed.

He touched the earth with the palm of his hand, just as he did when stroking the women that he had invented in his play acting. I fell to my knees and implored him again:

—*Brother, don't leave me all by myself.*

—*You don't understand, Mwanito. Where I'm going, there's no one else. I'm the one who's going to be all by myself . . . or don't you believe in your darling father any more?*

His tone was sarcastic: my brother was getting his revenge on me for being the favourite son. He pushed me away with a shove, and closed the doors behind him. I stood there, peeping through the cracks in the wood, my eyes full of tears. I wasn't just witnessing the departure of my only childhood companion. It was part of me that was leaving. As far as he was concerned, he was celebrating the beginning of all beginnings. As for me, I was being unborn.

And I saw how Ntunzi raised his arms in a "v" for victory, savouring his moment like a bird setting off skywards. He stayed for a time swaying backwards and forwards, deciding which way to go. As if he were teetering on the edge of a cliff. He danced around on the tips of his toes, as if he were expecting to take a plunge rather than a step forward. I wondered: why was he taking so long to set off? And then I had my doubts: could it be that he wanted that instant to last forever? Was he indulging himself in the joy of having a door, and being able to close it behind him?

But then something happened: instead of moving forward as he had intended, my brother doubled up as if he had been hit by some invisible blow behind the knees. He fell on his hands and lay down in the posture of a wild animal. He dragged himself over the ground in circles, snuffling amongst the dust.

I quickly vaulted over the fence to help. And it pained me to see him: Ntunzi was stuck to the ground and in tears.

—Bastard! You great son-of-a-bitch!

—What's wrong, brother!? Come on, get up.

—I can't. I can't.

I tried to lift him. But he weighed as much as a sack of stones. We still managed to stagger along, shoulder to shoulder, dragging ourselves as if we were wading against the current of a river.

—I'll call for help!

—What help?

—I'll try and find Uncle.

—Are you crazy? Go back home and bring the wheelbarrow. I'll wait here.

Fear dilates distances. Under my feet, the miles seemed to multiply. I reached the camp and brought the little handcart. This was the barrow in which my brother would be transported back home. Spilling over the cart on either side his legs swayed, hollow and lifeless like those of a dead spider, all the way home. Defeated, Ntunzi whimpered:

—I know what it is . . . It's bewitchment . . .

It was indeed bewitchment. But not a jinx put on him by my father. It was the worst of all spells: the one we cast on our own selves.

* * *

My brother fell ill again after his frustrated attempt at escape. He shut himself away in his room, curled up in bed and pulled the blanket up to cover himself completely. He stayed like that for days, his head hidden under the cover. We knew he was alive because we saw him shaking, as if he was having convulsions.

Little by little, he lost weight, his bones pricking his skin. Once again, my father began to get worried:

—Now son, what's the matter?

Ntunzi answered so quietly and peacefully that even I was surprised:

—I'm tired, Father.

—Tired of what? If you don't do anything from morning till night?

—Not living is what I find most tiring.

It gradually became clear: Ntunzi was going on strike over existing. More serious than any illness was this total abdication of his. That afternoon, my father lingered by his first-born's bed. He pulled back the blanket and examined the rest of his body. Ntunzi was sweating so profusely that his sheet was soaked and dripping.

—Son?

—Yes, Father.

—Do you remember how I used to tell you to make up stories? Well, make one up now.

—I haven't got the strength.

—Try.

—Worse than not knowing how to tell stories, Father, is not having anyone to tell them to.

—I'll listen to your story.

—You were once a good teller of stories, Father. Now, you're a story badly told.

I swallowed awkwardly. Although low in tone, Ntunzi's voice was firm. And above all, it had the assurance of the finality of things. My father didn't react. He hung his head and sank into himself as if he too had given up. One of us might be dying and it was his fault. Old Silvestre got up, turned and walked round and round the room until Ntunzi's whisper once again made itself heard:

—Brother Mwana, do me a favour . . . Go to the back wall and scratch another star in it.

I set off, aware that my father was following me. I made for the ruins of the old refectory and stopped only when I came to the huge wall that still preserved the black, scorched colour from when it had been set on fire. With a little stone, I drew a star on this big old wall. I heard my father's voice behind me:

—What the devil is this?

The darkened wall was covered with thousands of tiny stars that Ntunzi had scratched every day, like the work of a prisoner on the walls of his cell.

—This is Ntunzi's sky, each star represents a day.

I can't be sure, but my father's eyes seemed to fill with unexpected tears. Could it be that a dike had burst deep within him, and the grief of past ages that he had managed to contain for years was now bubbling up? I'll never be sure. For a moment later, he seized a spade and began to scrape the wall with it. Its metal blade re-emphasized the blackened layer upon which Ntunzi had recorded the passage of time. Silvestre Vitalício took his time over this labour of destruction. By the time he had finished, the surface was covered with a darkened squares, while he, exhausted, went back the way he had come like some black, scaly reptile.

UNCLE APROXIMADO

Someone says:
"There were roses here in the old days"
And so the hours
Melt away indifferently
As if time were made of delays.

Sophia de Mello Breyner Andresen

When he drove us to the camp eight years ago, the ex-Orlando Macara didn't believe that his brother-in-law, the future Silvestre, would remain so true to his decision to emigrate from his own life for good. Nor did he suspect that his name would be changed to Uncle Aproximado. Perhaps he preferred the form of address his nephews used for him previously: Uncle Godmother. None of this crossed our uncle's mind when he brought us to the reserve. It was late in the afternoon when Aproximado climbed down from the truck, and pointing at the wide expanse of bush, said:

—*This is your new home.*

—*What home?*— my brother asked, as his gaze swept across the untamed landscape.

My father, who was still sitting in the truck, corrected him:

—Not our home. This is our country.

In the beginning, Uncle even lived with us. He stayed for a number of weeks. Aproximado was a former game warden who had lost his job because of the war. Now that there wasn't even any world left, he had time to spend wherever he liked. For this reason, during the time he stayed with us, he put his hand to building and re-building the dwellings, repairing doors, windows and ceilings, bringing in sheets of corrugated iron and cutting down the vegetation around the camp. The savannah loves to gobble up houses and make castles unfit for human habitation. The earth's great mouth had already devoured some of the houses and deep cracks had opened up in walls like scars. Dozens of snakes had to be killed inside and in the vicinity of the ruined houses. The only building that wasn't rehabilitated was the administration block in the centre of the camp. This residence — which we came to call the "big house" — was cursed. It was said that the last Portuguese administrator of the reserve had been killed there. He had died inside the building and his bones must still be lying there among the rotting furniture.

During those first weeks, my old man was in a state of apathy, removed from the intense activity going on around him. He only busied himself with one task: making a huge crucifix in the small square in front of the big house.

—It's so that no one else can get in.

—But weren't you the one who told us we were the last ones alive?

—I'm not talking about the living.

As soon as he had nailed the sign to the cross, our old man summoned us all and, priest-like, conducted the ceremony of our re-baptism. That was when Orlando Macara ceased being our Uncle Godmother. His new designation indicated that he was not Dordalma's blood brother. He was, as Silvestre put it, a brother-in-law twice removed. He had been adopted at birth and for the rest of his life he would preserve his rank as an alien, foreign creature. Aproximado was able to talk with our relatives, but he could never converse with the family's ancestors.

Those first weeks came to an end, and our good Uncle went to live far away, pretending that he had settled in the guard's lodge at the entrance to the park. I always suspected that this was not his true residence. Ntunzi's frustrated flight had proved this: Aproximado's hiding place must be much farther away still, in the middle of the dead city. I imagined him scavenging among the ruins and the ash.

—*Not at all*— countered Ntunzi, —*Uncle really does live in the hut at the entrance. He's there under Father's orders, keeping watch.*

This was his job: he was there to protect his brother-in-law, in his isolation, given that he was guilty of killing our mother. Aproximado had his guns trained outwards and, who knows, maybe he'd already killed police who were trying to find Silvestre. That was why we would occasionally hear the sound of gunfire in the distance. It wasn't just the soldier Zachary shooting the animals that would be turned into our dinner at night. These shots were different, and had another purpose. Zachary Kalash was a second prison guard.

—*They're all in it together. In fact, those two are a three-some*— Ntunzi guaranteed. —*They're joined by blood, of course, but it's the blood of others.*

Wherever it was that he lived, the truth is that Aproximado only visited us in order to keep us supplied with goods, clothes, medicine. But there was a list of banned imports, at the top of which were books, newspapers, magazines and photos. They would have been old and out of date anyway, but in spite of this, they were prohibited. In the absence of images from Over There, our imagination was fed by stories that Uncle Aproximado would tell us when my father wasn't around.

—*Uncle, tell us, what's happening in the world?*

—*There is no world, my dear nephews, hasn't your father told you enough times?*

—*Go on, Uncle . . .*

—*You know, Ntunzi, you've been there.*

—*I left so long ago!*

This conversation annoyed me. I didn't like being reminded that my brother had once lived over there, that he had known our mother, and that he knew what women were like.

* * *

He didn't tell us about the world, but Aproximado ended up telling us stories, and, without him being aware of it, these stories brought us many different worlds rather than just the one. For Uncle, having someone paying him attention was reason enough for him to be grateful.

—*I'm always amazed that someone wants to listen to me.*

As he spoke, he moved around, now this way now that, and it was only then that we realized that one of his legs was skinnier and shorter than the other. Our visitor, and may I be forgiven for saying this, looked like the Jack of Clubs. Out of error or haste, he had been put together in a way that left no space for either his neck or his legs. He gave the impression of being so tubby that there were no points to his feet. And rotund as he was, he looked as tall when he was standing as when he was on his knees. He was timid, bowing formally and respectfully as if confronted by a low doorway whichever way he turned. Aproximado would speak without ever abandoning his modest ways, as if he were always mistaken, as if his very existence were no more than an indiscretion.

—Uncle, tell us about our mother.

—Your mother?

—Yes, please, tell us what she was like.

The temptation was too great. Aproximado went back to being Orlando, and warmed to the idea of travelling through the recollections of his half-sister. He looked all around him, checking on Silvestre's whereabouts.

—Where's that fellow Silvestre?

—He went to the river, we can talk.

So Aproximado coursed and discoursed. Dordalma, may God preserve her many souls, was the most beautiful of women. She wasn't dark like he was. She'd inherited her fair skin from her father, a little mulatto from Muchatazina. Our father got to know Dordalma and was smitten.

—Don't you think our father might yearn for her?

—Ah! Come on now: who knows what it is to have a yearning?

—Does he or doesn't he?

—To yearn for someone is to wait for flour to turn back into grain.

And he would ruminate on the meaning of what it is to yearn. Everything is in a name, he would say. Names, and nothing else. Let us take the butterfly, for instance: does it really need wings to fly? Or could it be that the very name we give it is a fluttering of wings? And that was how Aproximado slowly and elaborately spun his answers.

—Uncle, come back to earth, talk to us. Tell us: did Silvestre and Dordalma love each other?

At first, they got on together like wind and sail, scarf and neck. Occasionally, it has to be said, they would flair up in minor discord. Everyone knows what Silvestre is like: as obstinate as a compass needle. Little by little, Dordalma cloistered herself in her own world, sad and silent like an unpolished stone.

—So how did our mother die?

Here, there was no answer. Aproximado was evasive: at the time, he was away from the city. When he arrived home, the tragedy had already occurred. After receiving condolences, our father had this to say:

—A widower is just another word for someone who's dead. I'm going to choose a cemetery, a personal one where I can bury myself.

—Don't say such a thing. Where do you want to go and live?

—I don't know, there isn't anywhere any more.

The city had foundered, Time had imploded, the future had been submerged. Dordalma's half-brother still tried to make him see reason: he who leaves his place, never finds himself again.

—You haven't got any children, Brother-in-law. You don't know what it's like to surrender a child to this festering world.

—But have you no hope left, brother Silvestre?

—Hope? What I've lost is confidence.

He who loses hope, runs away. He who loses his confidence, hides away. And he wanted to do both things: to run away and to hide away. Nevertheless, we should never doubt Silvestre's capacity to love.

—Your father is a good man. His goodness is that of an angel who doesn't know where God is. That's all.

His whole life had been devoted to one task: to be a father. And any good father faces the same temptation: to keep his children for himself, away from the world, far from time.

* * *

Once, Uncle Aproximado arrived early in the morning, thus ignoring the instruction that he should only turn up in Jezoosalem at the end of the day. In normal circumstances, Uncle would stumble in his steps, and his legs seemed to obey two contrary urges.

—*If I'm limping it's not a defect but a precaution*— he would say.

This time, he'd thrown caution to the wind. Haste was the only ruler of his movements.

My father was busy patching up the roof of our house. I was holding the ladder where he was perched. Uncle twirled around and exclaimed:

—*Come down, Brother-in-law. I've got news.*

—*News finished long ago.*

—*I'm asking you to come down, Silvestre Vitalício.*

—*I'll come down when it's time to come down.*

—*The president has died!*

At the top of the steps, all activity stopped. But only for a few seconds. Then, I felt the ladder vibrating: my old man was starting to climb down. Once on the ground, he leant against the wall and busied himself wiping away the sweat that dripped from his face. My Uncle walked over to him:

—*Did you hear what I said?*

—*I did.*

—*It was an accident.*

Silvestre continued to wipe his face indifferently. With the palm of his hand, he shaded his eyes and looked up at where he had been perched.

—*I just hope that's plugged the leak*— he concluded, carefully folding the cloth he had cleaned himself with.

—*Did you listen to what I told you? That the president has died?*

—*He was already dead.*

And he went inside. Uncle Aproximado remained, kicking the stones in front of the house. Fury is just a different way of crying. I stayed away, pretending to put the tools away. No one should approach a man who is pretending not to cry.

Then, Aproximado made a sudden decision. He went over to the ammunition store and called for Zachary. They talked for a while in muffled tones at the door of the hut. The news left the old soldier in a state of shock. It wasn't long before he seized a rifle, beside himself with rage, and began to wave it around in the air threateningly. He crossed the little square in front of our houses, shouting repeatedly:

—*They killed him! The bastards, they killed him!*

And off he strode in the direction of the river, his cries growing ever fainter until the sound of cicadas could be heard once again. When everything seemed to have calmed down, my father suddenly opened the door of his room and addressed his brother-in-law:

—*See what you've done? Who told you to give him the news?*

—*I'll speak to whomever I like.*

—*Well you're not going to speak to anyone else in Jezoosalem.*

—*Jezoosalem doesn't exist. It's not on any map, only the map of your madness. There is no Silvestre, Aproximado doesn't exist, nor Ntunzi, nor . . .*

—*Shut your face!*

Silvestre's hands tugged at Aproximado's shirt. We were afraid of what would happen next. But the only substance old Vitalício gave his anger was when he made the following harsh pronouncement:

—*Get out of here, you little cripple! And don't come back, I've got no more orders for you.*

—*I'll take my truck and never come here again.*

—*And apart from anything else, I don't want motor vehicles passing this way, they churn up the soil and leave the earth with a gaping wound.*

Aproximado pulled his keys from his pocket and took his time picking out the one to unlock his truck. This delay was his dignified retort. He'd leave, but when he chose. Ntunzi and I ran to try and persuade him otherwise.

—*Uncle, please don't go!*

—*Have you never heard the proverb: he who wants to dress up as a wolf is left without any skin?*

We didn't understand the adage, but we did understand that nothing would deter him. When Uncle was already sitting in the driver's seat, he rubbed his forehead with his handkerchief as if he wanted to scrape off his skin or increase his already abundant baldness. And the roar of the truck drowned the sound of our farewells.

* * *

The following weeks flowed over us like a thick oil. Our food supplies gradually ran low and we began to depend almost exclusively on the meat that Zachary brought us, already cooked, at the end of the day. The garden produced little more than inedible grasses. Nameless wild fruits kept us going.

Meanwhile, Ntunzi busied himself drawing a new map and I spent whole afternoons down by the river as if its flow might cure me of an invisible wound.

One day, however, we heard the sound of the truck that we longed for so much. Aproximado had returned. In the little square, he braked with a flourish, sending up a cloud of dust. Without greeting us, he walked round the vehicle and opened its rear doors. Then, he began to unload boxes, crates and sacks. Zachary got up to lend a hand, but Silvestre's harsh words made him stop.

—*Sit down and stay where you are. None of this is for us.*

Aproximado unloaded the vehicle without any help. When he'd finished, he sat down on a box and gave a tired sigh:

—*I've brought you all this.*

—*You can take it back*— my father answered crisply. *No one asked you for anything.*

—*None of it is for you. It's all for the kids.*

—*You can take it all back. And you, Zaca Kalash, help load this junk back onto the truck.*

The assistant began by putting his arms round a box, but he didn't get as far as lifting it. Our Uncle, boosted by an unexpectedly loud voice, countermanded:

—*Stop it, Zaca!*— and turning to my old man, he begged: —*Silvestre, Silvestre, listen to me, please: I've got grave news to tell you . . .*

—*Has another president died?*

—*This is serious. I've noticed signs of life near the entrance.*

—*Signs of life?*

—*There's someone out there.*

We expected my father to deny everything outright. But he sat in silence, surprised by the fierceness of his brother-in-law's declaration. We were astonished when Silvestre pointed to the empty chair and said:

—*Sit down, but don't stay long. I've got lots to do. Have your say, then . . .*

—*I think the time has come. Enough is enough! Let's go back, Mateus Ventura, the kids . . .*

—*There's no Mateus here.*

—*Come away, Silvestre. It's not just the kids, I can't take this any more.*

—*If you can't take it, go away. You can all go. I'm staying.*

Silence. My father looked up at the sky as if he were seeking company for his future stay. Then, his eyes alighted slowly on Zachary Kalash.

—*What about you?* My father asked.

—*Me?*

—*Yes, you, Comrade Zachary Kalash. Do you want to stay or leave?*

—*I'll do what you do.*

Zachary spoke and there was nothing more to be said. He clicked his heels lightly and withdrew. Aproximado pulled up his chair next to Silvestre and sugared his voice for what he was going to say next.

—I need to understand, brother: why do you insist on staying here? Was it a problem at the Church?

—The Church?

—Yes, tell me, I need to understand.

—As far as I'm concerned, there has been no Church at all for a long time.

—Don't say that . . .

—I'll say it, and say it again. What's the point of having a belief in God if we've lost faith in men?

—Was it a problem with politics?

—Politics? Politics is dead, it was the politicians that killed it. Now, all that's left is war.

—Like this, there's nothing to talk about. You're going round in circles, rambling on and on.

—That's why I'm telling you: go away.

—Think of your sons. Above all, think of Ntunzi, who's ill.

—Ntunzi's better, he doesn't need your lies to get well . . .

—All this shit about Jezoosalem, it's all one big lie— Aproximado yelled, showing that the conversation was now over.

The visitor moved away, limping more than usual. He looked as if he was simultaneously falling on both sides. As if his shortage of breath heightened his congenital defect.

—Go and do your limping far away from here, you freak.

Silvestre took a deep breath, relieved. He needed to insult someone. It was true that he mistreated Zachary. But his assistant was a little man. What's the fun in insulting a little man?

ZACHARY KALASH,
THE SOLDIER

[...]
Things have long been lived:
In the air are extinct spaces
Shape recorded in emptiness
Of voices and gestures that were once here.
And my hands can grasp nothing.

Sophia de Mello Breyner Andresen

—*They'll pop out, I'll show you in a minute.*
Zachary's zealous fingers pressed the muscles of his leg
right back to the bone. Suddenly, bits of metal popped out of
his flesh, fell and rolled around on the ground.
—*They're bullets*— Zachary Kalash proclaimed proudly.
He picked them up one by one with the tips of his fingers
and revealed the calibre of each and the circumstances in
which he had been shot. Each of the four bullets had its own
particular origin.
—*This one, the one from the leg, I got in the Colonial War.
The one in the thigh, that one came from the war with Ian Smith.
This one, in the arm, is from the present war* . . .

—*What about the other one?*

—*What other one?*

—*The one in the shoulder?*

—*I don't remember that one.*

—*That's a lie, Zachary. Go on, tell us.*

—*I'm serious. I sometimes don't even remember the others.*

He wiped the projectiles on the sleeve of his shirt and stuffed them back in his flesh, using his fingers as if he were pushing in the plunger of a syringe.

—*Do you know why my bullets and I are inseparable?*

We knew. But we pretended we were hearing it for the first time. Just like the saying that he himself had invented and ceaselessly intoned: if you want to know a man, take a look at his scars.

—*They are the opposite of my navel. It was through here*— and he pointed to the holes —*it was through here that death escaped.*

—*Leave the bullets alone, Zaca, we want to know about other things.*

—*What other things? I only have the skills that animals have: I can sense death and blood.*

* * *

After my brother's convalescence, Silvestre Vitalício believed that radical change would have to occur in Jezoosalem. So he made a decision: Ntunzi and I went to live for a while with Zachary Kalash. It was to clear our minds and, at the same time, to learn the riddles of existence and the secrets of subsistence. If we ever lost Zachary, then we would replace him in the life-saving activity of hunting.

—*Make them wallow around in the mud*— my old man ordered.

It was envisaged that we would roam along isolated paths, learn the arts of tracking and hunting wild animals, master the secret languages of the trees. And yet Zachary abstained from his role as teacher. What he wanted was to tell stories about hunting, to talk without conversing, to listen to himself in order not to hear his own ghosts. But we demanded other topics of conversation.

—*Tell us about our past.*

—*My life is a mole's burrow: four holes, four souls. What do you want to talk about?*

—*About our mother, and how she and our father courted.*

—*No, certainly not. I'll never talk about that.*

Zachary's reaction seemed excessive. The man shouted, his hands crossed over his chest, and he went on and on without stopping:

—*No, never.*

He was the grandson of a soldier, the son of a sergeant, and he himself had never been anything but a soldier. So they shouldn't come to him with the heart's strategies, love and worthless yearning. Man is a creature with a taste for death, who loves Life, but likes even more to stop others from living.

—*You still feel you're a soldier. Own up to it, Zaca, do you miss the barracks?*

The fellow ran his hands lovingly over the military tunic he always wore. His fingers lingered sleepily on the barrel of his rifle. Only then did he speak: It's not the uniform that makes a soldier. It's the oath. He wasn't one of those who had enlisted because he was scared of Life. His being a soldier, as he put it, stemmed from the momentum of the moment. There wasn't even a word for soldier in his mother tongue. The term used was "massodja," and had been stolen from the English.

—*I never had any causes, my only flag was myself.*

—*But Zaca, don't you remember our mother?*

—*I don't like going back in time. My head doesn't have a long range.*

Ernie Scrap, now renamed Zachary Kalash, had encountered deaths and shoot-outs. He'd escaped crossfires, he'd escaped all his recollections. His memories had fled through all the perforations of his body.

—*I was never good at remembering. I've been like that since the day I was born.*

It was Uncle Aproximado who discovered why he was so forgetful: why didn't Zachary remember any wars? Because he'd always fought on the wrong side. It had always been like that in his family: his grandfather had fought against Ngungunyane, his father had enlisted in the colonial police, and he himself had fought for the Portuguese during the war of national liberation.

For our visiting relative, Uncle Aproximado, this amnesia was worthy of nothing save scorn. A soldier without a memory of war is like a prostitute who claims to be a virgin. That's what Aproximado, without mincing his words, told Zachary to his face. The soldier, however, turned a deaf ear and never answered back. With an angelic smile, he steered the conversation out into the vacuousness of a subject in which he felt at ease:

—*Sometimes I ask myself: how many bullets might there be in the world?*

—*Zaca, no one's interested in knowing about that . . .*

—*Could it be that during the war, there were more bullets than there were people?*

—*I couldn't tell you*— Ntunzi replied. —*Nowadays, you can be sure there are: six bullets are enough to exterminate mankind. Have you got six bullets?*

With a smile, Zachary pointed to the boxes. They were full of ammunition. There was more than enough to exterminate various mankinds. Everyone laughed except for me. For the emotion of living between the memories and forgetfulness of wars weighed heavily upon me. Gunpowder was part of our Nature, as the forgetful soldier assured us:

—*One day I'm going to sow my bullets. Plant them out there . . .*

—*Why did you leave the city, Zaca? Why did you come with us?*

—*What was I doing there? Digging holes in emptiness.*

And as he spoke, he spat. He apologised for his manners. He was a man of correct breeding. He merely spat in order to rid himself of his own taste.

—*I'm my own poison.*

At night, his tongue would unfold like a snake's. He would wake up with the taste of venom in his mouth, as if he'd been kissed by the devil. All because a soldier's slumber is a slow parade of the dead. He awoke just as he lived: so lonely that he talked to himself merely so that he wouldn't forget human speech.

—*But Zachary: don't you miss the city?*

—*Not at all.*

—*Don't you even miss someone?*

—*My whole life has been lived in war. Here is where I've found peace for the first time . . .*

He wouldn't go back to the city. As he said, he didn't want to depend on instructions for his income. We should watch and see how he survived in Jezoosalem: he slept like a guinea-fowl. On the branch of a tree for fear of the ground. But on the lowest branch, in case he fell.

* * *

Zachary Kalash didn't remember the war. But the war remembered him. And it tortured him with the renewal of old traumas. When there was thunder, he would rush out into the open in a frenzy, yelling:

—*Bastards, you bastards!*

All around him, the animals protested and even Jezebel whinnied in despair. They weren't complaining about the storm. It was Zachary's fury that upset them.

—*He gets like that because of the thunderclaps*— Silvestre explained. That's what frightened him: the memory of explosions. The clash of clouds wasn't a noise: it was the reopening of old wounds. We forget the bullets, but we never forget the wars.

* * *

Our father had sent us to live at the ammunition store and, for me, the real reason behind this had to do with Ntunzi and the need for him to be distracted. The natural hierarchy allotted Ntunzi a rifle and me a simple catapult. Zachary showed me how to improvise some elastic out of the truck's old tires, and to construct a weapon with a deadly reach. The stone was projected with a sudden hiss, and the bird plummeted to the ground, hit by its own weight. It was my stone of prey.

—*You kill, you eat.*

That was Zaca's command. But I wondered: can such a colourful little bird, so full of song, really be put on our dinner plate.

—*The only thing I can teach you and Ntunzi is not to miss your shot. Happiness is a question of aim.*

—*Don't you feel any pity when you kill?*

—*I don't kill, I hunt.*

The animals, he claimed, were his brothers.

—*One day, I'm the predator, next day, they're the ones who'll gobble me up*— he argued.

To be good at taking aim isn't a skill: it's an act of charity. In fact his aim was suicide: every time he killed an animal, it was he himself who was the target. And that morning, Zachary was once again going to have to shoot himself: our father had ordered us to bring some game for dinner.

—*Uncle Aproximado is coming and we want to welcome him with plenty to eat and drink.*

That was why we set off into the bush in pursuit of a

bushbuck, the antelope that barks and bites like a dog. The soldier went on ahead and transmitted orders to us with his hands. From time to time, Zachary would pause and get down on his knees. Then, he would dig a little hole, crouch down and speak into the opening, whispering inaudible secrets.

—*The earth will tell me where the hoofed animals are.*

And once again off we would go, following trails that only Zachary seemed to know about. It was almost noon and the heat drove us to find some shade. Ntunzi collapsed on the ground and satisfied his somnolence and fatigue.

—*Wake me up one of these days*— he begged.

What happened next took me by surprise: the soldier got up and turned his coat into a pillow to make Ntunzi more comfortable in his sleep. I had never imagined such attention possible in Jezoosalem. Returning to the shade of the agbagba tree, Zachary slowly prepared a cigarette, as if he got more pleasure from rolling it than smoking it. He gradually settled down by the trunk and, satisfied, gazed far up into the foliage.

—*This tree goes very well with the soil*— he said.

The catapult lay dormant in his hand, which was nevertheless aware of every shifting shadow. The birds spend all their time flitting about. The hunter never really relaxes. Half his mind, that feline side of him, is ever watchful.

—*Always a hunter, eh?*

—*What? Just because of this catapult? No, this is just to make me feel like a child.*

And he seemed to vacillate in the face of sleep, so exhausted that he didn't seem to want to move his eyes. The sun was at its peak, and merely having a body represented an unbearable burden.

—*Did you ever have a wife, Zaca?*

—*I was always hopping around from here to there, never settling down in my mind. This world, my son, only provides a perch for vultures.*

As far as we knew, the soldier had never had a wife or a son. Kalash explained himself. Some people are like firewood: good to be next to. Others are like eggs: always in dozens. That wasn't the case with him. He was like the bushbuck: always wandering devoid of any company. It was a habit he'd got from the wars. No matter how big the platoon, a soldier always lives alone. Soldiers die collectively, and are buried in more than a common grave: they're buried in a common corpse. But when it comes to living, they do it alone.

* * *

In the shade of the agbagba, we all seemed to have succumbed to sleep. But suddenly, the soldier leapt up as if impelled by some internal spring. He aimed his rifle and a shot tore through the silence. There was a noise among the bushes and we tumbled after it, in a dash to recover the wounded antelope. But the creature wasn't where we expected. It had escaped through the vegetation. A trail of blood on the ground indicated the path it had taken. That was when we witnessed an unexpected transformation in Kalash. Ashen faced, he stumbled and to stop himself falling, he sat down on a stone.

—*You two follow the trail.*

—*All on our own?*

—*Take the rifle. You, Ntunzi, do the shooting.*

—*But aren't you going with us, Zachary?*

—*I can't.*

—*Are you ill?*

—*I was never able to do it.*

Was that experienced hunter and veteran soldier of so many wars balking at the last shot? Then Zachary explained that he was incapable of facing up to blood and the death throes of his prey. Either the shot hit the target and death was immediate, or he repented and gave up.

—Blood makes me behave like a woman, but don't tell your father . . .

Ntunzi took the rifle and not long afterwards, we heard shots. Soon he re-emerged dragging the animal behind him. From that day on, Ntunzi developed a taste for gunpowder. He would get up before dawn and trek through the bush, as happy as Adam before he lost his rib.

***

While Ntunzi was learning to be a hunter again, I was the one who got the most pleasure from being a shepherd. First thing in the morning, I would take the goats out to pasture.

—All the earth is a road for goats. And every piece of ground is pasture. There isn't a wiser animal— Zaca remarked.

A goat's wisdom lies in imitating a stone in order to live. On one occasion, when I was helping to herd the animals back into the corral, Zachary confessed something: there was, in fact, a memory that kept coming back to him. It went like this: Once, during the Colonial War, he watched an injured soldier being brought in. Nowadays, he knows: soldiers are always wounded. War even injures those who never get to the front. Well, this soldier was no more than a kid, and his injury was this: every time he coughed, a torrent of bullets came out of his mouth. That cough was contagious: he needed to get away. Zachary didn't just feel the need to get away from the barracks. He wanted to emigrate from the time of all wars.

—It's just as well the world has ended. Now I get my orders from the bush.

—And from Father?

—With all due respect, your father is part of the bush.

I was going in the opposite direction to Zaca: one day soon, I'd be an animal. How could it be that we were still men when we were so far from people? That was my question.

—Don't think about it. It's back there in the city that we begin to behave like animals.

At the time, I didn't realize how right the soldier was. But now I know: the more uninhabitable the world gets, the more people live in it.

* * *

I had long ceased to understand Zachary Kalash. My doubts began over the question of his former name. Ernie Scrap. Why Scrap? It was obvious: he was a scrap of a human being, an anatomical leftover, a surplus bit of soul. We knew, but we never spoke of it: Zachary had been downsized as a result of a landmine going off. The contraption exploded, and trooper Scrap took off, like some primitive imitation of a bird in flight. They found him weeping, unable to walk. They sought in vain for physical injury. But the explosion had damaged his entire soul.

My doubts about Zachary's humanity went further, however. On moonless nights, for instance, he would fire his rifle into the air, as if in celebration.

—What am I doing? I'm making stars.

Stars, he claimed, are holes in the sky. The countless stars were nothing more than this, holes that he opened up, shooting into the dark target of the firmament.

On the most starry nights, Zachary would call us out to see the heavenly spectacle. We would complain, dozily:

—But we're sick of seeing . . .

—You don't understand. It's not for you to see. It's for you to be seen.

—Is that why you sleep outside the house?

—That's for other reasons.

—But isn't it dangerous, sleeping outdoors like this?

—I was an animal once. And I'm still learning to be a person.

We didn't understand Jezoosalem, Kalash claimed.

—*Things here are people*— he explained.

We complained that we were alone? Well, everything that was around us were people, humans turned into stones, into trees, into animals. And even into a river.

—*You, Mwanito, should do what I do: greet things when you pass by them. That way you'll feel at peace. That way, you'll be able to sleep outdoors, anywhere you like.*

My night-time fears would be dissipated if I began to say hello to bushes and boulders. I never got to test the truth of Zachary Kalash's advice for the simple reason that he withdrew shortly afterwards.

* * *

It happened straight after the unexpected appearance of Uncle Aproximado. Late in the afternoon we heard footsteps near the ammunition store, and Zachary crept forward, his weapon raised, ready to fire. The soldier whispered to my brother:

—*It's an injured animal, it's limping; you do the shooting, Ntunzi . . .*

Then we heard our Uncle's unmistakable voice from behind the shrubs:

—*Do the shooting like hell! Calm down, it's me . . .*

—*I didn't hear the truck*— he said.

—*It broke down at the entrance. I've had to come all the way up here on foot.*

Aproximado greeted us, sat down in the shade, and drank. He took his time, and then spoke:

—*I've come from Over There.*

—*Have you brought stuff?*— I asked inquisitively.

—*Yes, but that's not what I've come about. I've come with news.*

—*What is it, Uncle?*

—*The war has ended.*

He filled his water bottle and went back to the camp. We later heard the noise of the truck fading into the distance. Once silence had descended, Zachary ordered Ntunzi to return his weapon. My brother refused vehemently:

—*It was Father who told me to do training . . .*

—*Your father's in charge of the world, I'm in charge of the weapons.*

Kalash's voice had changed, the words seemed to grate in his throat. He put the weapon away in the ammunition store and locked the building. Then we saw him go to the well and lean over as if he wanted to throw himself into the abyss. He stayed there for half an hour. Afterwards, he stood up straight again, apprehensive, and merely told us:

—*Go back to the camp, I'm going . . .*

—*Where are you going?*

He didn't answer. Then we heard the soldier walk away, treading on dry leaves.

***

Zachary withdrew and no one saw him for days. We settled back in our room and there we remained as if time had become nothing more than waiting. There was no sign of Aproximado and no indication of the soldier's whereabouts. We didn't even hear any shots in the distance.

Then, one day, when I was taking tobacco leaves to Jezebel, I came across Zachary lying in the corral, with a thick beard and smelling more strongly than a wild animal.

—*How're you doing, Zachary?*

—*I left without any meaning, and came back without any means.*

—*Father wants to know what you've been doing there shut away for so long?*

—*I'm building a girl. It's taking so long because she's a foreigner.*

—*So when do you see yourself finishing?*

—*She's done, now all she needs is a name. Now go away, I don't want any living person round here.*

—*Is that what he said?*— My father enquired when I got back to the camp. Silvestre asked me to reproduce, word for word, my conversation of a few moments earlier with the soldier. The furrow in my old man's brow grew deeper. Everyone suspected that Zachary possessed secret powers. We knew, for example, how he could fish without a net or a line. With the skill of Christ, he would wade into the river until the water reached his waist. Then, still advancing, he would plunge his arms into the water for a few seconds and withdraw them loaded with jumping fish.

—*My body's my net*— he would say.

The following day, Zachary returned to his duties, now recovered and wearing his uniform. My father didn't ask him anything. The daily routine of Jezoosalem seemed to have been re-established: the soldier would leave early in the morning, his rifle strapped to his back. Occasionally, we would hear shots in the distance. My father would allay our fears:

—*It's just Zachary with his craziness.*

It wasn't long before the assistant burst into view, carrying an animal that had already been butchered. But then we began to hear the sound of gunfire at times when Zachary was with us.

—*Who are the people doing the shooting now, Father?*

—*Those shots are echoes of old ones.*

—*What do you mean, Father?*

—*It's not happening now. They're echoes of a war that's over now.*

—*You're mistaken, Silvestre my friend*— Zachary declared.

—*What do you mean mistaken?*

—*No war ever ends.*

JEZEBEL THE JENNY

Anguish for being me and not another.
Anguish, my love, for not being she
who gave you many daughters, married a virgin
and at night readies herself knowing
she's the object of love, attentive and fair.

Anguish for not being the great island
to hold you and not drive you to despair.
(Night approaches like a wild creature)

Anguish for being water in the midst of earth
and for my anxious, mobile mien.
And at once multiple and immobile

Not knowing whether to leave or await you.
Anguish for loving you, if it moves you.
For being water, my love, while wishing I was soil.

Hilda Hilst

F inally, let me introduce you to our last member of humanity: our beloved donkey, Jezebel by name. The jenny was
the same age as me, which was old for an animal of her species.

And yet, Jezebel was, as my father put it, in the flower of her youth. The secret behind her elegance lay in the tobacco she chewed. This delicacy was ordered through Uncle Aproximado and shared between Zachary and the jenny. Late in the afternoon, one of us would take her whole leaves and the donkey would rejoice at the sight, trotting over happily to receive her greens. Ntunzi once remarked how he found it amusing to watch the movements of her thick lips.

—*Thick? Who said they're thick?*

That was my old man jumping to Jezebel's defence. More than the tobacco, it was the love that Silvestre devoted to the donkey that explained why she was so gorgeous. No one had ever seen such respect paid in a case of zoological affection. He would court her every Sunday. It must be said that only my father had any idea what day of the week it was. Sometimes we had a Sunday on two consecutive days. It depended on the state of his needs. But the fact was that on the last day of the week, everyone knew for sure what would happen: bearing a bouquet of flowers, and wearing a red tie, Silvestre would make his way solemnly to the corral. The fellow was parading himself to fulfil what he termed "the will of the unwilled." At some distance from the corral, my old man would respectfully announce himself:

—*May I come in?*

The donkey would turn round, with an imperceptible flutter of her eyelashes, and my father would pause, hands resting on his stomach, waiting for a signal. We never found out what this signal might be. But the truth was that in due course, Silvestre would express his gratitude:

—*Thank you so much, Jezebel, I've brought you these humble flowers . . .*

We would watch the donkey chew the bunch of flowers. And then, my father would disappear inside the corral. And that was that.

* * *

One particular Sunday, things can't have gone according to plan. Silvestre returned from his love tryst in a rage. He carried his fury on the tip of his foot and his curses on the tip of his tongue. Head bowed, he kept saying:

—*It's never happened to me before, never, never! Really never.*

He strode round the room, kicking the few bits of furniture. His impotent, repressed anger caused his voice to tremble:

—*It's a curse put on me by that bitch!*

We almost took him literally: the bitch, by association, must be Jezebel. But no. The bitch was his late wife. My mother. My ex-mother. The disruption to Vitalício's manly functions had been caused by Dona Dordalma's spell.

Having lowered himself into his chair on the veranda, my father sought my services as a tuner of silences. It was the end of the afternoon, and shadows darted around taking over the world. Silvestre was like one of these shadows: fleetingly still. But it wasn't long before he jumped up suddenly and ordered:

—*Come with me to the corral!*

—*What are we going to do?*

—*I'm going to do*— he corrected. —*I'm going to apologize to Jezebel. So the poor girl isn't sad, thinking it was her fault.*

I remained at the entrance to the corral, saw my father hug the jenny's neck, and then the surrounding darkness enveloped me. An inner rage prevented me from watching. I was aflame with jealousy for Jezebel. On our way back, a flash lit up the savannah and a huge crash of thunder deafened us. The November rains were beginning. It wouldn't be long before Zachary emerged to insult the gods.

That same night, father ordered us to go and guard the corral. What about Zachary? We asked. Why not send for the person whose job it was to undertake this duty?

—*That fellow's useless when there's thunder. You two go, and take the torch.*

Jezebel was agitated, whinnying and kicking. And it wasn't because of Zachary's foul-mouthing, for he was quiet and keeping to himself inside his hut. It must be for some other reason and it was our mission to find out why she was so agitated. Ntunzi and I walked out under the intense thunder. The jenny looked at me with an almost human appeal, her ears pointing down in fear. There was an intermittent gleam in her velvet eyes, like flashes of lightning from within her soul.

Ntunzi sat down sleepily while I tried to soothe the animal. She began to calm down, her flank nestling up to my body, seeking comfort and support. I heard my brother's malicious comment:

—*She's getting all come-hither, Mwanito.*

—*Come off it, Ntunzi.*

—*Go on, mount the broad.*

—*I didn't hear you.*

—*You heard me only too well. Go on, undo your fly, the broad fancies you.*

—*Come on, brother, Jezebel's scared, that's all.*

—*You're the one that's scared. Go on, Mwanito, take your trousers off, nobody would think you're the son of Silvestre Vitalício.*

Ntunzi came over and pushed me, forcing me to lean over the jenny's back, while I begged him:

—*Stop it, stop it.*

Suddenly, in amongst the trees, I glimpsed a moving shadow, creeping along, cat-like. Terrified, I pointed to it:

—*A lioness! It's a lioness!*

—*Let's get out of here, quick, give me your torch . . .*

—And Jezebel? Are we going to leave her here?

—To hell with the bloody donkey.

Then suddenly, we heard a shot. It seemed more like a flash of lightning, but a second shot left us in no doubt. Our soldier was right: faced with a shot, whether it hits or misses, we all die. Occasionally, some lucky ones return amid the dust raised by fright. That's what happened to us. In the confusion, Ntunzi tripped over me and both of us, covered in mud and flat on the ground, peered through the grass. Zachary had hit the prowling lioness.

The feline creature managed to stagger drunkenly a few steps, as if death were a fit of giddiness that caused you to end up on the ground. Then, it collapsed, with a fragility that didn't match its regal stature. The moment the lioness fell to the ground, it stopped raining. Zachary made sure it was really dead, and then fell to his knees and addressed the heavens, praying the wound caused in him by his shot might be healed.

My father appeared, all in a hurry, and he didn't stop with us. He walked along the fence looking for Jezebel, and when he found her, he stopped to comfort her.

—Poor thing, she's trembling all over. Tonight, she's going to sleep in the house.

—In the house?— Ntunzi asked, astonished.

—She'll sleep there tonight and as many nights as are necessary.

She only slept there that night. That was enough for Ntunzi to vent all his jealous feelings when he addressed me:

—He never let you, his own son, in there, but the donkey's allowed to sleep inside . . .

***

After the accident, the corral was moved nearer. The moment night fell, bonfires were lit all around it to protect the jenny from the covetousness of any predators.

Weeks passed until one day Silvestre decided to call another meeting. Hurriedly, we gathered in silence in the square with the crucifix. Uncle Aproximado, who happened to have spent the night with us, also lined up next to me. With a stern frown, the old man looked each one of us in the face, peering unhurriedly into our eyes. Finally, he growled:

—*Jezebel's pregnant.*

I just wanted to laugh. The only female among us had ful-filled her natural function. But my old man's icy look killed off any desire in me to make light of it. A sacred rule had been violated: a seed of humanity had come through victorious and threatened to bear fruit in one of Jezoosalem's creatures.

—*This is how all the whorishness of the world will begin again.*

—*But with respect, Brother-in-law*— said Aproximado, —*couldn't it be that you are the father?*

—*I take precautions, you know that very well.*

—*Who knows, maybe once, by accident, in the height of passion . . .*

—*I've already told you it wasn't me*— bellowed my old man.

His anger was upsetting him so much that his mouth was-n't big enough for all his saliva and his spittle was like a shower of meteorites:

—*There's only one truth: she's pregnant. And the bastard who did it is here, among us.*

—*I swear, Silvestre, I've never even looked at Jezebel*— the soldier, Zachary, declared forcefully.

—*Who knows whether it's not just some swelling she's got from an illness?*— Aproximado queried, timidly.

—*It's an illness caused by some son-of-a-bitch who's got three dangly bits between his legs*— my old man snarled.

I kept my eyes to the ground, incapable of facing my father's passion for the jenny. His repeated threats followed us as we went back to our rooms:

—Whoever it was, I'll twist his nuts off!

* * *

A month later, Zachary raised the alarm: since the early hours, Jezebel had been bleeding and twisting about, whimpering and kicking. At first light, she gave a last shudder. She seemed to have died. But she had just squeezed out the foetus. Zachary held the new claimant to life, and lifted it up in his arms, covered in blood and mucus. The soldier proclaimed in a restrained tone:

—This is a son of Jezoosalem!

The moment we got the news, we all met at the corral, crowding round the still breathless jenny. We wanted to see the newborn creature, concealed among its mother's thick fur. We never got as far as entering the corral: our father's tempestuous arrival put an end to our eager expectation. Silvestre ordered us to keep away, he wanted to be the first to face the intruder. Zachary presented himself with military punctiliousness at the gate to the corral:

—Take a look at the baby, Silvestre, and you'll see who the father is straight away.

Silvestre penetrated the gloom and vanished for a while. When he re-emerged, he looked perturbed, his quick step betraying his turbulent mind. Barely had our father disappeared than we burst in on the jenny's resting place and knelt down by her side. The moment our eyes got used to the darkness, we saw the furry creature lying next to Jezebel.

The black and white stripes, though not clearly defined, gave the game away: the father was a zebra. Some fierce stallion had paid our place a visit and courted his distant relative. Ntunzi took hold of the newborn animal and caressed it as if it were human. He gave it affectionate names and walked up and down, cradling it like a mother. I never thought my brother capable of such tenderness: the little creature settled in his arms and Ntunzi smiled as he murmured:

—*Well, let me tell you something my little baby: your dad has left my old man with a broken heart.*

Nor did Ntunzi realize how right he was. For not long afterwards, Silvestre returned to the corral, seized the baby from the arms that were holding him and issued his order, to be carried out immediately and decisively:

—*I want you to bring me that old zebra, balls and all, do you hear, Zaca?*

* * *

That night, my father went to the corral and took the baby donkey-zebra in his hands. Jezebel followed his movements with tears in her eyes, while Silvestre kept repeating, as if intoning some chant:

—*Oh, Jezi, why did you do this to me? Why?*

He seemed to be caressing the newborn babe. But in fact what his hands were doing was smothering the fragile creature, the tiny zebra mulatto. He took the now lifeless little animal in his arms and set off far from the corral. He buried it himself, down by the river. I watched him carry out this act, incapable of intervening, incapable of understanding. That awful deed would forever be a sticking point in any thoughts I might have about our father's generosity. Ntunzi never came to know what had happened on that night. He always believed that the babe had died of natural causes. Nature in its ferocity had reclaimed the stripes on an ass not born in the wild.

When he had filled the grave, Silvestre Vitalício went down to the waters. Following him at some distance, I assumed he was going to wash his hands. It was then that I saw him drop to his knees. Was he weakening, struck by some internal flash of light? I drew nearer, wanting to help, but fear of punishment made me hide from being seen. It was then that

I realized: Silvestre Vitalício was praying. Even today, a shudder runs through me when I recall that moment. For I don't know whether I'm inventing it, or whether I really remember his supplication: "My God, protect my sons as I have proved unable to protect myself. Now that I don't even have angels, come to Jezoosalem to give me strength . . . ."

Suddenly, my father became aware of my presence. He changed his submissive posture, shook his knees and asked:

—*Are you trying to give me a fright?*

—*I heard a noise, Father. I came to see if you needed any help.*

—*I was feeling the soil: it's still dry. If only it would rain more.*

He cast his eyes up into the clouds pretending to look for signs of rain. Then he sighed and said:

—*Do you know something, son? I committed a terrible mistake.*

I thought he was going to confess to his crime. So my father was going to redeem himself, absolved by having confessed his remorse.

—*So what was this mistake, Father?*

—*I never gave this river a name.*

This was his confession. Perfunctory, without emotion. He got up and put his hand on my shoulder.

—*You choose a name for this river, son.*

—*I don't know, Father. A name is too big a thing for me.*

—*Very well, I'll choose one then: it's going to be called the River Kokwana.*

—*I think that sounds pretty. What does it mean?*

—*It means "grandfather."*

I shuddered: was my father weakening in his prohibition against any mention of ancestors? So delicate was the moment that I didn't say anything for fear that he might retreat from his decision.

—*Your paternal grandfather used to pray on the banks of rivers when he wanted to ask for rain.*

—And afterwards, did it rain?

—It always does rain afterwards. What happens is that the prayer may be said too far in advance.

And he added:

—The rain is a river guarded over by the dead.

Who knows whether the recently named river might not fall under the command of my paternal grandfather? And who knows too whether I might not feel less lonely precisely for this reason?

I returned to my room, where my brother's little reading lamp was still alight. Ntunzi was drawing what looked to me like a new map. There were arrows, no entry signs, and incomprehensible scribbles that looked like the Russian alphabet. In the middle of this map, there it was, in all its serene certainty, a ribbon coloured in blue.

—Is it a river?

—Yes, it's the only river in the world.

And then suddenly, the paper turned to water, and the floor was covered in thick drops. Avoiding the puddle that covered the floor, I sat down on a corner of his bed. Ntunzi cautioned me:

—Mind your feet don't get wet, this is dripping all over the place.

—Ntunzi, tell me something: what's a grandfather like?

To my great envy, Ntunzi had known the whole range of grandparents. Maybe it was out of shame that he'd never spoken of them. Or who knows, perhaps it was for fear that my father might find out? Silvestre Vitalício forbade memories. The family was us, and no one else. The Venturas had no past and no future.

—A grandfather? Ntunzi asked.

—Yes, tell me what one's like.

—A grandfather or a grandmother?

It didn't matter. In fact, it wasn't the first time I'd asked him this question. And my brother never answered me. He kept counting on his fingers as if the idea of such progenitors required elaborate calculations. Whatever he was doing, he was counting the uncountable.

That night, however, Ntunzi must have completed his tally. For he returned to the subject without prompting, when I was already tucked up in bed. His hands cupped an emptiness, with great care, as if he were carrying a tiny bird

—*Do you want to know what a grandfather is like?*

—*I kept asking you, you never gave me an answer.*

—*You've never seen a book, have you, Mwanito?*

And he explained to me what this alluring object was made of, comparing it to a huge pack of cards.

—*Imagine cards the size of your hand. A book is a pack of these cards, all stuck together down one side.*

His look became vague as he passed his hand over this imaginary pack of cards and he said:

—*If you caress a book like this, you'll know what a grandfather is like.*

His explanation left me disappointed. I found the idea of a grandfather commanding rivers much more attractive. We were almost asleep when I remembered something:

—*By the way, Ntunzi, I've nearly finished the pack of cards.*

—*What do you mean finished? Have you lost the cards?*

—*No, it's not that. There's no space left for writing.*

—*I'll find you something to write on. I'll see to it tomorrow.*

* * *

The following day, Ntunzi pulled out from under his shirt a bundle of coloured papers, and said tersely:

—*You can write here.*

—*What's this?*

—*It's money. They're notes.*

—*What am I going to do with it?*

—*Do what you did with the cards, write wherever there's a bit of clear space.*

—*So where did you find this money?*

—*How do you think our uncle manages to get hold of the things he brings us?*

—*He tells us they're just bits and pieces he picks up in places that have been abandoned.*

—*You don't know anything, my little brother. You're old enough to be fooled, but I'm now old enough to be swindled.*

—*Can I write now?*

—*No, not now. Hide this money away in case Father catches us . . .*

I concealed the notes under my sheet as if I were spiriting away some company for my dreams. When Ntunzi was already snoring and I was alone, my fingers trembled as they caressed the money. Without knowing why, I put the painted papers to my ear to see if I could hear voices. Was I doing what Zachary did when he listened to his holes in the earth? Who knows whether those old notes didn't contain hidden stories?

But the only thing I could hear was the drumbeat of my fearful heart. This money was my old man's most secret possession. Its presence was incontrovertible proof that he had been lying all along. Over There was after all, alive and well, and governed Jezoosalem and its living souls.

BOOK TWO

THE VISIT

That which they call "dying" is merely to stop living and what they call "being born" is to begin dying. And that which they call "to live" is to die while living. We don't wait for death but live with it perpetually.

Jean Baudrillard

THE APPARITION

I want a licence to sleep,
an excuse to rest for hours on end,
without even dreaming
the slightest wisp of a tiny dream.

I want what before life
was the deep sleep of all species,
the dignity of a state.
A seed.
Much more than roots.

                                        Adélia Prado

We never really get to live during most of our life. We waste ourselves in a boundless lethargy that we delude and console ourselves by calling existence. For the rest, we flit around like fireflies, lit up only for brief and intermittent moments.

A whole life can be turned on its head in one day by one such moment. For me, Mwanito, it happened on that day. It began in the morning, when I left the house in the face of a windstorm that was raising spirals of dust everywhere. These whirlwinds would twist and turn in whimsical dances, only to cease as phantasmagorically as they had begun. The foliage of the huge trees swept the ground while heavy branches were torn away and fell to the earth with loud crashes.

—*No one go outside . . .*

Those were my father's orders, as he peered out of the window, tormented by the storm and its gusts of wind. Nothing disturbed Silvestre Vitalício more than to see trees twisting and great branches full of leaves swinging like ghostly serpents.

Disobeying my father's orders, I ventured down the paths between our living quarters and the big house. And I regretted doing so straight away. The storm was like the upheaval of all the compass points at the same time. I felt a chill run through me: was there any basis for my old man's fears? What was happening? Was the ground tired of being earth? Or was God announcing his arrival at Jezoosalem?

With my left hand shielding my face and my right holding the two sides of my old coat together, I walked down the path until I stopped in front of the ghostly residence. I stood there for some time without moving, listening to the whistling of the wind. I was reassured by its howling: I was an orphan and the wind was wailing mournfully, like someone seeking its lost relatives.

In spite of the discomfort, I savoured my misbehaviour as revenge against Silvestre Vitalício. Deep down, I wanted the storm to worsen so as to punish our progenitor for his wrongdoings. I felt like going back and challenging old Vitalício in front of the very window through which he watched this cosmic insubordination.

Meanwhile, the gusts of wind increased in fury. So much so that the front door of the big old house was blown open. This was a signal for me: an invisible hand was inviting me to

98

cross the forbidden threshold. I went up the front steps and peered at the veranda where hundreds of leaves were pirouetting in a frenzied dance.

Suddenly, I saw the body. Stretched out on the ground, a human body. I was overwhelmed by an inner turmoil. I cast an anxious glance once again to confirm what I had seen. But a heaving sea of leaves blurred my vision. My legs trembled, rooting me to the spot. I must have been mistaken, it was my imagination, and nothing more. Another gust, another swirl of dead leaves and, once again the vision returned, this time more clear and real. It certainly was a body, lying there on the veranda like top soil.

I ran away, shrieking like one possessed. As I was running into the wind, it swallowed up my screams, and it was only when I got back to the house, breathless, that I was able to give vent to my distress:

—*A person! A dead person!*

Silvestre and Ntunzi were mending the handle of a spade and didn't stop their task. My brother looked up, his eyes betraying no interest:

—*A person?*

I clumsily gave hurried details of what I had seen. My father, impassive, commented quietly:

—*This fucking wind!*

Then, he put his hammer down and asked:

—*What did its tongue look like?*

—*Its tongue?*

—*Was it sticking out of its mouth?*

—*Father: it was dead, it was far away. I couldn't see its mouth, nor its tongue.*

I sought some sort of understanding in Ntunzi, but he didn't say a word. But given my conviction, Father issued his orders:

—*Call Zachary over here.*

Ntunzi left in a rush. It wasn't long before he returned with the soldier carrying, as always, his rifle. My old man got things moving with a couple of words:

—Get yourself over there and see what's happening . . .

Zachary saluted, clicked his heels, but didn't obey immediately. He squared himself to request due permission to speak:

—May I say something?

—You may.

—Mwanito can't have seen what was really there. It was an optical disillusion.

—That may be— Silvestre conceded. —But it may also be one of those old dead bodies in the house. Some animal may have dragged it out onto the veranda.

—That's possible. Last night there were hyenas prowling around.

—Quite so. If that's the case, bury it. Bury the body, but not underneath a tree.

—But won't you want to know who it is?

—If it's a dead body, it can't belong to anyone. Go and see to the task, and if the wind dies down, I'll come and join you . . .

—Maybe he was living here in Jezoosalem, and we didn't know— Ntunzi suggested, with unexpected daring.

—Are you mad? If there is a body there, it's not that of anyone who died. It's someone who was always dead, born lifeless, so to speak.

—Father, I'm sorry, but for me . . .

—That's enough! I don't want to hear any more opinions. You're going to dig a grave and that body, or whatever it is, is going to be put away in the earth.

Ntunzi, Zachary and I set off in single file, in a pre-funeral cortège. We still heard Silvestre's voice, summing up his conclusions:

—Later, when the wind drops, I'll go and check things.

The soldier marched along in front, a spade in each hand. We stealthily climbed the steps up to the big house, and to my relief, my previous vision was confirmed. Half-covered by leaves, perfectly clear against the light, there lay a body. Some hidden force rooted us to the doorway, until Kalash murmured:

—*I'll go and take a look!*

—*Don't go in, Zaca!*— Ntunzi warned.

—*Why?*

—*I don't like that light*— and he pointed to a sunbeam that filtered through the roof planks.

Sitting on the entrance steps, Zachary sniffed the air, as if trying to detect a suspicious smell.

—*It doesn't smell of death*— he said in a cavernous tone that made us shiver.

And once again, we peered towards the end of the veranda trying to see through the light that shone from the rear.

—*It's a man*— he said, sure of himself.

The body lay on its back on the wooden floor, as if the floor were the suggestion of a coffin. We couldn't see the face that was turned to the other side. A kind of cloth covered the head, tied at the back.

—*It looks*— Zaca said —*like a foreign black.*

—*How do you know?*

The body wasn't embracing the ground like local corpses do. Those bones weren't seeking another womb in the earth. There was, of course, the detail of the boots. Zachary had never seen the like of them before.

—*Now I'm beginning to think it's a white*— Zaca declared, still peering from the top of the steps. —*I think the fellow's soul has already begun to leave its shell.*

And he gave the order for us to dig the grave, before any-thing else. When it was ready, we'd go back and fetch the body. By that time, the light on the veranda would have changed and we would be protected by bad spirits.

So we began to dig, our spades opening up the stranger's final resting place. But then a strange thing happened: the hole was never ready. The moment we got to the bottom, the windblown sand completely refilled the grave again. And that happened once, twice, and three times. The third time, Zachary hurled his spade at the ground as if he'd been stung by a wasp and exclaimed:

—I don't like this. Children, come over here quickly.

And he pushed us towards the shade of a mafurreira tree. He took a white cloth from his pocket and tied it to the trunk. His hands were shaking so hard that it was Ntunzi who spoke:

—I know what you're thinking, Zaca. I feel the same too.

Then, turning to me, he said:

—This is what happened at our mother's funeral.

—It's the same spell— Zachary confirmed.

Then they told me what had happened on the day of my mother's burial. "Burial" is merely a term that is used. For there's never enough earth to bury a mother.

—I don't want a gravedigger.

That was Silvestre's stipulation, which he yelled in order to be heard above the wind. The dust stung his eyes. But he didn't lower his eyelids. His tears protected him from the clouds of dirt.

—I don't want a gravedigger. My son and I are the ones who'll dig the grave, we're the ones who'll do the funeral.

But the grave they started was never finished. My father and Ntunzi tried, time after time, in vain. Hardly had they opened up a hole than it filled with sand. Kalash and Aproximado joined in, but the result was the same: the dirt, blown by the wind in its fury, refilled the cavity immediately. They had to resort to the professionals to complete the job of opening and closing the burial place.

Now, eight years later, the earth was once again refusing to open its womb to receive a body.

—*Quiet everyone!*— ordered Zachary Kalash. —*I can hear noises.*

Taking every possible care, the assistant approached the veranda. He peered between the planks and then turned towards us in astonishment. Where before the corpse had lain, there was nothing whatsoever.

—*The dead body isn't there any more, it's nowhere to be seen*— Zachary repeated in an undertone.

The wind had abated. Even so, dead leaves fluttered around accentuating the emptiness.

—*I'm going to get a weapon*— Zaca said. And he hurried away down the path.

Gradually, a new state of mind took hold of me, transforming my fright into a haughty sense of calm. I looked at Ntunzi who was trembling like a reed, and to his astonishment, I began to advance firmly towards the big house.

—*Are you crazy, Mwanito? Where are you going?*

In silence, I climbed the steps to the veranda and trod on the boards carefully in case the floor were to give way, and I were to fall through it and maybe even join the missing dead body. I walked along the veranda looking for some clue, until I decided to knock on the front door. My brother, his voice shaking, asked:

—*Are you waiting for the dead man to come and answer the door?*

—*Don't talk so loud.*

—*You're crazy, Mwanito. I'm going to call Father*— Ntunzi said, turning his back and retreating hurriedly.

I was alone, facing the abyss by myself. Slowly, I opened the door and peered around the entrance hall. It was a wide, empty space, which smelled of time stood still. While I was getting used to the half-light, I began to think to myself: why was it that through all my childhood years I was never curious enough to come and explore this forbidden place? The reason was that I had never had control over my own childhood, my father had made me grow old from the time I was born.

It was then that the apparition occurred: out of the nothingness, there emerged a woman. A crack opened up by my feet and a billowing cloud of smoke misted my eyes. The vision of this creature suddenly caused the frontiers of the world I knew so well to overflow.

I faced the intruder out of the corner of my half-closed eyes. She was white, tall and dressed like a man, in trousers, a shirt and high boots. She had straight hair, half concealed under a kerchief, the same one we had seen on the head of what we had thought a dead body. The boots were also identical to the ones that the dead person was wearing. Her nose and lips were blurred, and together with the colour of her skin, gave her the appearance of an unburied creature.

I wanted to run away, but my legs were like the roots of an ancient tree. Without moving my head, I glanced at the ill-defined approach to the house, seeking help. There was nothing. Neither Ntunzi nor Zachary could be seen, and the land round about was shrouded in mist. Bewildered, I felt a tear weigh more than my whole body. That was when I heard the woman speak for the first time:

—*Are you crying?*

I shook my head energetically. I thought that if I owned up to my weakness, this would merely encourage the spectre in its demonic intentions.

—*What are you looking for, my child?*

—*Me? Nothing.*

Did I speak? Or were they words that came out of me without my being aware? For I was completely defenceless, barefoot on burning ground. All of a sudden, I no longer knew how to live. Life had turned into an unknown language.

—*What's the matter, are you scared of me?*

The gentle, tender voice only aggravated my sense of unreality. I brushed my eyes with my hand to wipe away the tears and then slowly raised my face to assess the creature. But always out of the corner of my eye, for fear that the vision might tear my eyes out forever.

—*Was it you who were digging a grave in the yard just now?*

—*Yes. Me and the others. There were lots of us.*

—*I could hear voices and took a look. Why were you digging a grave?*

—*It wasn't for anyone. I mean, for anything.*

I turned my gaze to the veranda once more, anxiously trying to discover what had happened to the body. There was no sign on the floor that it had been dragged away, for the leaves were scattered around without having been disturbed. The intruder passed by me, and I was aware, for the first time in my life, of the sweet smell of a woman. She moved away towards the front door. I noticed the graceful way she walked, but without the exaggerated gestures with which Ntunzi had imitated female creatures in his play-acting.

—*I beg your pardon, but are you really a woman, miss?*

The stranger raised her eyes, troubled by some age-old pain. There was a passing cloud, and then she shook off her sadness and asked:

—*Why? Don't I look like a woman?*

—*I don't know. I've never seen one before.*

That was my first woman and she made the ground melt away under me. Since then, years have passed, I've fallen for countless women, and whenever I've loved them, the world has always sunk from under my feet. But that first encounter etched the mysterious power of women into my consciousness.

Feeling my strength return, I rushed off like a gazelle through the bush. The white woman observed me from the doorway, intrigued. I even looked back, hoping that she might have vanished, wishing it had all been no more than a hallucination.

When I reached the safety of home, my heart was pounding, so much so that I could scarcely utter a word when I found Ntunzi:

—*Ntunzi, you . . . you won't believe this.*

—*I saw it*— he said, as startled as I was.

—*What did you see?*

—*The white woman.*

—*Did you really see her?*

—*We mustn't say anything to Father.*

* * *

That same night, my mother visited me. In my dream, she was still faceless, but now she had a voice. Her voice was that of the apparition, with its warmth and tenderness. I woke up confused, so vivid was the dream. I heard steps in the room: Ntunzi couldn't sleep. He had also been accosted by nocturnal visitations.

—*Ntunzi, tell me something: was our mother like her?*

—*No.*

—*Why couldn't you sleep, Ntunzi?*

—*I was having dreams.*

—*Were you dreaming of Mama as well?*

—*Do you remember that story of the girl who lost her face when I fell in love with her?*

—*Yes. But what's that got to do with it?*

—*In my dream, I saw her face.*

The sound of voices outside made us stop talking. We rushed to the window. It was Zachary, speaking to our father. Judging by his gestures, we guessed the soldier was reporting the apparition. So we watched Zachary gesticulating, explaining in an animated fashion what had happened at the haunted house. My father's expression became more and more grim: we were being visited, the earth and the heavens were shaking in Jezoosalem.

All of a sudden, Silvestre got up and vanished into the darkness. We followed him from afar, keen to discover what was going on in the man's mind as he crossed the yard like a wounded animal. Silvestre went straight to the truck and shook Aproximado, who was snoozing in the front seat. There was no warning, or even a greeting:

—*What's this white woman doing here?*

—*She wasn't the only one to arrive. Why don't you ask me what I'm doing here?*

Overcome with emotion, my father signalled to Kalash to come over. Silvestre looked as if he wanted to confide something, but no word came out of his mouth. Suddenly, he started kicking Aproximado, while the soldier tried in vain to shield our Uncle. And so the three of them spun around together, like the broken blades of a windmill. Finally, my father leaned against the front of the vehicle, exhausted, and took a deep breath, as if he were trying to regain entry to his soul. His voice was like that of Christ on the cross, as he asked:

—*Why did you betray me, Aproximado? Why?*

—*I've got no obligations towards you.*

—*Aren't we family?*

—*That's what I sometimes ask myself.*

He'd said too much. Aproximado had crossed the line. My father stood there speechless, huffing like Jezebel after her trot. And then he watched, stunned, as Aproximado unloaded a whole range of odds and ends from his truck: binoculars, powerful torches capable of drilling through the night, cameras, sun hats and tripods.

—*What's all this? An invasion?*

—*It's not all that much. The lady likes to take photos of herons.*

—And you tell me it's "not all that much"? Someone in this world is going round taking photos of herons?

This was just an additional reason for his discomfort. The truth was that the presence of the Portuguese woman in itself was an unbearable intrusion. One person alone — and a woman to boot — was bringing the entire nation of Jezoosalem to its knees. In just a few minutes, Silvestre Vitalício's painstaking fabrication was falling to pieces. There was, after all, a living world out there, and an envoy from that world had installed herself at the very heart of his realm. There was no time to lose: Aproximado was to pack up everything once more and take the intruder back where she had come from.

—You, Brother-in-law, are going to take this broad away!

Aproximado smiled, sly and sardonic, which is what he did when he couldn't think of what to say. He steadied his body inside his overalls, mustering up the courage for an argument:

—My dear Silvestre: we're not the owners.

—We're not what? Well, I'm the owner of all this, and I'm the only current occupant of this whole area.

—Well, I don't know about that . . . Can't you understand that maybe it's us who'll have to leave?

—Why's that?

—The houses we're occupying are the property of the State.

—What State? I don't see any State around here.

—One can never see the State, Brother-in-law.

—It's for that and other reasons that I got out of that world where the State can never be seen, but it always turns up and takes our things away from us.

—You can shout, Silvestre Vitalício, but you're here illegally . . .

—Illegal is the bitch who bore you . . .

He was so enraged that he lost control of his voice, which sounded like a cloth being ripped in half. We'd never seen him reach such a state. My father set off in the direction of the administrator's house, and started yelling:

—*You bitch! You great bitch!*

He projected his whole body forward as if the words he was hurling were stones:

—*Get out of here, you bitch!*

Seeing him duelling with the void like this made me feel sorry for him. My father wanted to shut the world away. But there was no door behind which to lock himself.

* * *

It was early in the morning when my old man came to my bedside and shook me. He leaned over my pillow and whispered:

—*I've got a mission for you, son.*

—*A what, Father?* I asked, startled.

—*A spying mission*— he added.

My task was an easy one and explained to me in two brief brush strokes: I would go to the big house and rummage through whatever was in the Portuguese woman's room. Silvestre Vitalício wanted to discover clues that might reveal the visitor's secret intentions. Ntunzi would have the job of distracting the woman, keeping her far from the house. And I wasn't to be afraid of shadows or ghosts. The Portuguese woman had already scared any tormented souls away. Local ghosts didn't get on well with foreign ones, he assured me.

Later on, halfway through the morning, the Portuguese woman's effects emerged into the light of day in my trembling hands. For hours, my eyes and fingers ranged over Marta's papers. Each sheet was a wing with which I gained giddiness rather than height.

THE WOMAN'S PAPERS

That which memory loves, remains eternal.
I love you with my memory, which never dies.

Adélia Prado

I'm a woman, I'm Marta and all I can do is write. Maybe, after all, it's best that you are away from here. For I could never reach you otherwise. I have long ceased to occupy my own voice. If you came to me now, Marcelo, I would be speechless. My voice has emigrated to a body that once was mine. And when I listen to my voice, I don't even recognize myself. When it comes to love, I only know how to write. This isn't recent, it's always been like that, even when you were present.

I write just as birds compose their flight: without paper, without script, with only light and nostalgia. Words that, while mine, have never dwelt in me. I write without having anything to say. Because I don't know what to say to you about what we were. And I have nothing to say to you about what we shall be. For I'm like the inhabitants of Jezoosalem. I feel no yearning, I have no memory: my belly has never borne life, my blood has never opened into another body. This is how I grow old: dispersed within me, a veil abandoned on a church pew.

I loved you, and you alone, Marcelo. My fidelity led me into the most painful of exiles: this love removed me from all possibility of loving. Now, of all the names, all I have left is your name. I can only ask that name what I used to ask of you: to beget me. For I need so much to be born! To be born another, far from me, far from my time. I am exhausted, Marcelo. Exhausted but not empty. To be empty, one must have internal substance. And I have lost my inner being.

Why did you never write? It's not reading you that I miss. It's the sound of the knife slitting the envelope that carries your letter. And once again feeling my soul caressed, as if somewhere an umbilical cord was being cut. But it was just an illusion: there is no knife, there is no letter. Nothing, or nobody, is being delivered into the world.

* * *

Do you see how small I become when I write to you? That's why I could never be a poet. A poet grows when faced by absence, as if absence were his altar, and he became greater than the word. That's not the case with me, for absence submerges me, so that I no longer have access to myself.

This is my conflict: when you're here, I don't exist, I'm ignored. When you're not here, I don't know myself, I'm ignorant. I only exist when I'm in your presence. And I am only myself in your absence. Now, I know. I'm no more than a name. A name that only comes to life when uttered by you.

* * *

This morning I watched the bushfire in the distance. On the other side of the river, vast stretches were being consumed. It wasn't the earth that was turning to flame: it was the air itself that was burning, the whole sky was being devoured by demons.

Later, when the blaze had died down, a sea of dark ash remained. In the absence of wind, particles fluttered around like black dragonflies over the scorched grassland. It could have been a scene from the end of the world. But for me, it was the opposite: it was the earth being born. I felt like yelling your name:

—Marcelo!

My cry could have been heard far away. For here, in this place, even silence produces an echo. If there is somewhere I can be reborn, it's here, where the briefest moment leaves me sated. I'm like the savannah: I burn to live. And I die, drowned by my own thirst.

* * *

—What's that word?

At the last stop before we reached Jezoosalem, Orlando (who I've got to get into the habit of calling Aproximado) asked, pointing at my name on the cover of my diary:

—What's that word?

—This woman— I corrected him. This is me.

I should have said: that's my name, written on the cover of my diary. But no. I said it was me as if my whole body and my whole life were contained in a mere five letters. That's what I am, Marcelo: I'm a word, you write me by night, and by day you erase me. Every day is a sheet you tear off, I'm the paper that awaits your hand, I'm the letter that awaits the caress of your gaze.

* * *

What struck me right from the start at Jezoosalem was the absence of electricity. Never before had I felt the night, been embraced by darkness, embraced inside me until I too became dark.

Tonight, I'm sitting on the veranda, under a star-filled

sky. Under the sky, no. In fact I'm among the sky. The firmament is so close, I could sow it with seeds, and I breathe slowly for fear of disturbing constellations.

The smell of the oil lamp burning is the only thing anchoring me to the ground. All the rest are indefinable vapours, unknown odours, angels whirling around me. Nothing precedes me, for I am inaugurating the world, light, shadow. More than this: I am founding words. I'm the one who launches them, I am the creator of my own language.

All this, Marcelo, reminds me of our nights in Lisbon. You would watch me in bed, while I rubbed beauty creams over my body. You complained there were too many: a lotion for the face, another for the neck, one for the hands, still another for around the eyes. They had been invented as if each part of me were a separate body and sustained its own particular beauty. As far as the sellers of cosmetics are concerned, it's no longer enough that each woman has her body. Each one of us has various bodies that exist in a kind of confederation of autonomous states. That's what you said as you sought to dissuade me.

Haunted by the fear of ageing, I allowed our relationship to grow old. Busy making myself beautiful, I allowed my true beauty, that which dwells in a candid look, to escape. The bed sheet grew cold, the bed played safe. That's the difference: the woman you met over there, in Africa, is beautiful only for you. I was beautiful for me alone, which is another way of saying for no one.

This is what these black women have that we can never have: they are always their whole body. They live in every part of their body. Their whole body is woman, their time is feminine. While we white women live in a strange state of transhumance: sometimes we are soul, other times we are body. We aspire to soar on the wings of desire, only to then crash to the ground under the weight of our guilt.

Now that I've got here, suddenly, I don't want to find you anymore. For me, it was a strange sensation, I who had travelled so far in my dream of reconquering you. But on my journey to Africa, this dream faltered. Perhaps I had waited too long. During my wait, I had learned to enjoy my yearning. I remember the verses of the poet, which go like this: "I came into the world to feel yearning." As if I could only populate my mind through absence. Following the example of those houses that can only speak to the senses when they are empty. Like this house where I now live.

* * *

The pain of a fruit that has fallen to the ground, that's what I feel. The portent of the seed, that's what I await. As you can see, I am learning how to be both tree and earth, time and eternity.

—*You're like the earth. That's your beauty.*

That's what you used to say. And when we kissed and I became breathless, I would ask you, between sighs: what day were you born? You would reply, your voice shaking: I'm being born now. And as you brought your hand up between my legs, I would ask you again: where were you born? And, almost voiceless, you would reply: I'm being born in you, my love. That's what you said. You were a poet, Marcelo. I was your poetry. And when you wrote to me, what you told me was so beautiful that I would get undressed to read your letters. I could only read you when naked. For it wasn't through my eyes that I received you, but with my whole body, line by line, pore by pore.

* * *

When I was still in the city, Aproximado asked me who I was, and I seemed to talk for the whole night. I told him everything about us, I told him almost everything about you, Marcelo. At one stage, perhaps because I was tired, I realized how surprised I was with the story I was telling. Secrets are fascinating because they were made in order to be revealed. I revealed secrets because I can no longer bear to live without fascination.

—*You know, Miss Marta: the journey to the reserve is very dangerous.*

I didn't answer, but the truth is that I was only interested in travel if it involved crossing infernos, passing my soul through conflagrations.

—*Tell me about this Marcelo. Your husband.*

—Husband?

I'm used to this: women explain themselves to themselves by talking about their men. While if it were you, Marcelo, explaining me to other men, your words would transform me into a simple creature to be contained in the speech of one man alone.

—*Last year, Marcelo came on a journey to Africa.*

He came with the illusions of those who have lived in a place: on a pilgrimage to nostalgia. He stayed here for a month and when he returned, he had changed out of all recognition. Perhaps it was his re-encounter with this land that had unsettled him. It was in Mozambique that he fought as a soldier years before. He thought he had been sent to an unfamiliar land in order to kill. But he had been sent to kill a distant country. During that fatal operation, Marcelo had ended up being born as another person. Fifteen years later, it wasn't the country he wanted to see again, but that process of birth he had gone through. I told him not to go. I had a strange foreboding about his journey. No memory can be revisited. Even more serious: there are memories that are only re-encountered in death.

* * *

I've told you this, Marcelo, because the pain of it all is like that of an ingrown nail. I need to talk, to gnaw this nail right down to the skin. You don't know, Marcelo, how many deaths you made me die. For you came back from Africa, but part of you never returned. Every day, early in the morning, you would leave the house and wander the streets as if there was nothing you recognized in your city.

—*Is this city no longer mine?*

That's what you would say to me. A land is ours just as a person may belong to us: without our ever taking possession. A few days after your return, I found a photo at the bottom of your drawer. It was a picture of a black woman. She was young, pretty, her pensive eyes defying the camera. On the back of the photo, there was a note in tiny handwriting: a telephone number. The miniature writing made it look like the merest scratch. But it was an abyss I kept falling back into repeatedly, every time I emerged from it.

My first impulse was to make a phone call. But I thought twice about it. What would I say? Then my fury prevailed, uncontained. I threw the photo back, face down, like one might do with a corpse one didn't want to see the face of.

—*You cheat, I hope you die of AIDS, and with fleas along with it . . .*

I wanted to mistreat you, Marcelo, I wanted to throw you in jail. So you would remain shackled to my rage. I was past caring about love. I spent endless, sleepless nights, waiting. I waited for you to return so that I could talk to you, but when you arrived, you were too exhausted to listen. You'd be less tired the next day. Then, when the next day came, you phoned me from the airport to say you were leaving again for Mozambique. For the first time, I was surprised by my own tone of voice. And I told you: "Well then, sleep . . ." Just that. When what I wanted to say was: "Go and fuck your black girls once and for all." My God, how ashamed I am of my anger and of how spiteful my emotions made me.

I remained in Lisbon, dominated by the part of me that had gone with you. It was a sad irony that the person who kept me company the most during your absence was your lover. The photograph of the other woman stared at me from the bedside table. And we would contemplate each other, day and night, as if we had been forever joined by some invisible connection. I would sometimes whisper my decision to her:

—*I'm going to go and find him . . .*

But then your black mistress would counsel me: "Don't go!" Let him sink in the dark mud by himself. I convinced myself of the irrevocable truth: my husband had disappeared forever, a victim of cannibalism. Marcelo had been devoured, just as had happened to others who'd left for darkest Africa. He had been swallowed up by a huge mouth, a mouth the size of a continent. He had been gobbled up by ancient mysteries. There are no longer any savages, only natives. But natives can be beautiful. Above all, native women can be beautiful. And it is from that beauty that their bygone savagery emerges. It is a savage beauty. White men, in the past oppressors who were fearful of being devoured, nowadays want to be eaten, swallowed up by black beauty.

That's what your mistress told me. How many times did I fall asleep with my rival's photo in the margins of my slumber. Every time, I would mutter between my teeth: cursed woman! And I was never able to come to terms with the injustice of my fate. For years, I had paid considerable attention to makeup, diet, workouts in the gym. I had assumed that this was the way to continue to captivate you. It's only now that I've come to understand that seduction lies elsewhere. Perhaps in a look. And I had long ago allowed my fervent gaze to fade.

As I contemplated the fire sweeping across the savannah, I missed that exchange of fire, the mirror of bedazzlement in Marcelo. To bedazzle, as the word suggests, should be to blind, to take away the light. So it was a glaring light that I now sought. That hallucination that I had once felt, I knew, was as addictive as morphine. Love is a type of morphine. It could be turned into a commercial product, packaged with the name: Amorphine.

The so-called "women's magazines" sell recipes, secrets and techniques for how to love more and better. Little hints on how to enjoy sex. At the beginning, I was sold on this illusion. I wanted to win back Marcelo and I was open to any persuasion. Now, I don't know: all I want to know about love is precisely not to know, to disconnect the body from the mind, and allow it uncontrolled freedom. I'm just a woman in appearance. Underneath my surface expression I'm a creature of nature, a wild beast, a lava flow.

* * *

All this sky reminds me of Marcelo. He used to tell me, "I'm going to count stars," and then he would touch each of my freckles. He would dot my shoulders, my back, my breast with his finger. My body was Marcelo's sky. And I never discovered how to fly, to surrender to the languorous way he counted the stars. I never felt at ease with sex. Let's say it was a strange territory, an unknown language. My demureness was more than just shame. I was a deaf translator, incapable of turning the desire that spoke deep within me into outward expression. I was the rotten tooth in a vampire's mouth.

And so I return to my bedside table, to look your black mistress in the face. This was the gaze, at the moment the photo was taken, that plunged into my man's eyes. A luminous gaze, like the light at the entrance to a house. Maybe it was precisely that, a bedazzling look, maybe that's what

Marcelo had always desired. It wasn't sex after all. But to feel desired, even if it were only a fleeting pretence.

Under an African sky, I become a woman once more. Earth, life, water are my sex. No, not the sky, for the sky is masculine. I feel the sky touching me with all its fingers. I fall asleep under Marcelo's caress. And in the distance, I can hear the words of the Brazilian singer, Chico César: "If you look at me, I gently surrender, snow in a volcano . . . ."

I want to live in a city where people dream of rain. In a world where rain is the greatest happiness of all. And where we all rain.

. * * *

Tonight, I carried out the ritual: I stripped off all my clothes in order to read Marcelo's old letters. My love wrote so profoundly that, as I read, I felt his arm brush against my body, and it was as if he were unbuttoning my dress and my clothes were falling to my feet.

—*You're a poet, Marcelo.*

—*Don't say that again.*

—*Why?*

—*Poetry is a mortal illness.*

Marcelo would fall asleep straight away after making love. He would fold the pillow between his legs and sink into slumber. I was left alone, awake, to ruminate over time. At first, I considered Marcelo's attitude intolerably selfish. Then, much later on, I understood. Men don't look at the women they've made love to because they're scared. They're scared of what they may find in the depths of women's eyes.

EVICTION ORDER

I no longer fear myself. Farewell.

Adélia Prado

Marta's papers were burning my hands. I tidied them away so as no one could see that the intimacy inhabiting them had been violated. I returned home with a heavy heart. We fear God because he exists. But we fear the devil more because he doesn't. What made me more afraid at that particular moment was neither God nor the devil. I was especially worried about Silvestre Vitalício's reaction when I told him that all I had found in the Portuguese woman's room was a bunch of love letters. There was my old man at the entrance to the camp, hands on hips, his voice laden with anxiety:

—*A report! I want a report. What did you find in the Portagee woman's things?*

—*Just papers. That's all.*

—*So what did they say?*

—*Don't you remember, Father, that I can't read?*

—*Did you bring any papers with you?*

—*No. Next time . . .*

He didn't let me finish. He ran out of the kitchen and returned, the next moment, pulling Ntunzi by his arm.

—*You two go to the Portuguese woman's house and give her my order.*

—*What order, Father?*— Ntunzi asked.

—*You mean to say you don't know?*

We were to tell her to go back to the city. We were to be curt, we were to be gruff. The Portagee was to get the message fairly and squarely.

—*I want that woman out of here, far away, and I don't want to see her back here again.*

I looked at Ntunzi who was standing there, motionless, as if he were giving in. But within him, he must have been seething with recalcitrance. Nevertheless, he said nothing, and expressed no objection. There we stood, waiting for Silvestre to start speaking again. My father's silence kept both of us quiet and so we set off, meek and vanquished, in the direction of the haunted house. Halfway there, I asked:

—*Are you going to send the Portuguese woman away? How are you going to tell her?*

Ntunzi shook his head sluggishly. The two extremes of impossibility had met within him: he couldn't obey, but nor could he disobey. In the end, he said:

—*You go and speak to her.*

And he turned his back. I went on towards the big house, my steps faltering, like someone in a funeral procession. I found the intruder sitting on the steps, with a bag at her feet. She greeted me affectionately and stared up at the sky as if preparing to launch herself into flight. I expected to hear her say things in the gentle tone with which she had visited me in my dream. But she remained quiet while she took something from the bag, which I later learned was a camera. She took a photo of me, glimpsing hidden corners of my soul that I never knew existed. Then she took a small gadget made of metal from a case, and put it to her ear, only to put it away again.

—*What's that?*

121

She explained that it was a cellphone, and told me what it was for. But right there, in Jezoosalem, she couldn't pick up a signal for her machine.

—*Without this*— she said, pointing at the phone, —*I feel lost. My God, how I need to talk to someone . . .*

A deep sadness clouded her eyes. She looked as if she was going to burst into tears. But she controlled herself, her hands stroking her cheeks. And then she became distant for a while. She seemed to be muttering Marcelo's name. But it was so slow and quiet that it sounded more like a prayer for the dead. She slowly put everything away in her bag, and eventually asked:

—*Where do herons usually gather round here?*

—*There are lots in the lake*— I said.

—*When it's less hot, will you take me to this lake?*

I nodded. I didn't tell her about the crocodile that lived on the banks of the pond. I was afraid she might have second thoughts. At that moment, she began to rub creams into her body. Intrigued, I surprised her with a question:

—*Do you want me to go and get a bucket of water?*

—*Water? What for?*

—*Aren't you washing yourself?*

Her sadness was suddenly shattered: the Portuguese woman laughed out loud, and almost offended me. Wash? What she was doing was applying creams to herself as protection against the sun. Maybe she's got some illness, I thought. But no. The woman said that nowadays, sunlight was poisoned.

—*Not here, lady, not here in Jezoosalem.*

The Portuguese woman leaned on a wooden beam, closed her eyes and began to sing. Once again, the world escaped me. Never before had I heard a melody like that, flowing from human lips. I'd heard birds, the breezes and rivers, but nothing resembling her tones. Maybe in order to save myself from this lullaby, I asked:

—*Pardon me, but are you a whore?*

—*What?*

—*A whore—* I said slowly and deliberately.

At first astonished, and then amused, the woman lowered her head as if deep in thought, and in the end, she answered with a sigh:

—*Maybe, who knows?*

—*My father says all women are whores . . .*

She seemed to smile. Then she got up and, giving me an intense look, her eyes half-closed, exciaimed:

—*You're like your mother.*

A kind of flood rushed over my inner self as her gentle voice spread out and covered my entire soul. Some time was needed before I could ask myself: did this foreign woman know Dordalma? How and when had the two women met?

—*Begging your pardon, but do you . . .*

—*Call me Marta.*

—*Yes, lady.*

—*I know your family's story, but I never met Dordalma. And you, did you ever know your mother?*

I shook my head, as slowly as my sadness allowed me to control my own body.

—*Do you remember her?*

—*I don't know. Everyone says I don't.*

I wanted to ask her to sing once more. For there was something I was now sure of. Marta wasn't a visitor: she was an emissary. Zachary Kalash had predicted her arrival. As for me, I had a suspicion: Marta was my second mother. She had come to take me home. And Dordalma, my first mother, was that home.

* * *

The shadows were already lengthening when I accompanied Marta to the lake where the herons could be found. I helped her carry her photographic equipment and chose the paths down the slope that were less steep. Every so often, she would pause in the middle of the path, and with both hands, gather her hair together at the nape of her neck as if she wanted to avoid its obscuring her field of vision. Then, she would once again survey the firmament. I remembered Aproximado's words: "He who seeks eternity should look at the sky, he who seeks the moment, should look at the cloud." The visitor wanted everything, sky and cloud, birds and infinities.

—*What magnificent light*— she repeated, ecstatic.

—*Aren't you scared it might be poisoned?*

—*You can't imagine how much I need this light at this precise moment . . .*

She spoke as if in prayer. For me, the magnificent light was that which emanated from her movements. Nor had I ever seen such smooth, abundant hair. But she was talking of something that had always been there, and that I had never noticed: the light that radiates not from the sun but from places themselves.

—*Back there our sun doesn't speak.*

—*Where's "there," Miss Marta?*

—*Back there, in Europe. Here, it's different. Here the sun moans, whispers, shouts.*

—*Surely*— I commented delicately, —*the sun is always the same.*

—*You're wrong. There, the sun is a stone. Here, it's a fruit.*

Her words were foreign even though they were spoken in the same language. Marta's idiom was of another race, another sex, another type of smoothness. The mere act of listening to her was, for me, a way of emigrating from Jezoosalem.

At one point, the Portuguese woman asked me to turn away: she took off her blouse and let her skirt fall to the ground. Then, she went for a swim in her underwear. With my back to the river, I noticed Ntunzi, hiding in the undergrowth. His signal suggested that I should pretend I hadn't seen him. From his hiding place, my brother's eyes bulged with desire as he indulged his fire. For the first time, I saw Ntunzi's face go up in flames.

* * *

My father guessed right away that we hadn't carried out his instructions. To our astonishment, he didn't get angry. Was it that he understood our plausible excuses, did he condone our reticence, the clouds that blocked out the sun? He went and got changed into his best clothes, put on the same red tie he sported on his visits to Jezebel, the same dark shoes, the same felt hat. He took each of us by the hand, and dragged us along with him to the haunted house. He knocked on the door, and the moment the Portuguese woman answered it, he blurted out:

—My sons have disobeyed me for the first time . . .

The woman contemplated him serenely and waited for him to continue. Silvestre lowered his voice, softening his initial harsh tone:

—I'm asking you a favour. On behalf of myself and my two legitimate offspring.

—Come in. I'm afraid I don't have any chairs.

—We're not going to stay long, lady.

—My name's Marta.

—I don't call a woman by her name.

—What do you call her by, then?

—I won't have time to call you anything. Because you're leaving here right now.

—My name, Mister Mateus Ventura, is like yours: a kind of illness inherited from birth . . .

On hearing his former name, my father was struck by an invisible whiplash. His fingers squeezed my hand, as tense as a crossbow's arc.

—I don't know what you've been told, but you're mistaken, my dear lady. There's no one by the name of Ventura here.

—I shall leave, don't worry. What brought me to Africa is now almost over.

—And may I know what brought you here?

—I came looking for my husband.

—Let me ask you something, lady: you came so far just to look for your husband?

—Yes, do you think I should be doing more?

—A woman doesn't go looking for her husband. A woman stays and waits for him.

—Well in that case, maybe I'm not a woman.

I looked at Ntunzi in despair. The stranger was stating that she wasn't a woman! Was she telling the truth, and therefore contradicting the maternal feelings that she had inspired?

—Before setting out on my journey, I heard your story— Marta declared.

—There is no story, I'm here enjoying a short holiday in this exclusive retreat . . .

—I know your story . . .

—The only story, my dear lady, is the story of your departure, back to where you came from.

—You don't know me, a woman isn't only motivated by a husband. In life, there are other loves . . .

This time, my father was decisive in stopping her, by raising his arm. If he was allergic to anything, it was to conversations about love. Love is a territory where orders can't be issued. And he had created a little hideaway which was governed by obedience.

—This conversation has been dragging on for too long. And I'm an old man, lady. Every second I waste, I lose a whole Life.

—So you've finished saying what you came to say?

—That's all. You said you came looking for someone. Well, you can be on your way, because there's no one here . . .

—My dear Ventura, there's one thing I can tell you: you were-
n't the only one to leave the world . . .

—I don't understand . . .

—What if I were to tell you that we are both here for the same
reason?

It was painful to watch. She, a woman, a white
woman, and she was defying my old man's authority, showing up his weakness as a father and as a man in front of his
sons.

Silvestre Vitalício excused himself and withdrew. Later,
he explained that his anger was already overflowing, the
magma in the crater of a volcano, when he brought the conversation to an end:

—Women are like wars: they turn men into animals.

* * *

After his confrontation with the visitor, my father couldn't get
a good night's sleep. He tossed around in a minefield of nightmares and we listened to him, amid incomprehensible excla-
mations, calling, at one moment, for our mother, and at
another for the donkey:

—My little Alma! Jezebel, my sweet!

The following morning, he was burning with fever.
Ntunzi and I stood round his bed. Silvestre didn't even
recognize us.

—Jezebel?

—Father, it's us, your sons . . .

He looked at us with a pained expression and lay
there, his smile frozen on his face, his eyes expressionless,
as if he'd never seen us before. After a while, he placed his
hand on his chest as if to lend support to his voice, and
arraigned us:

—That's what you wanted, isn't it?

—We don't understand— Ntunzi said.

—*Did you want to take charge of me? Is that what you wanted, to see me struck down, to be able to bury me in my moment of weakness? Well I'm not going to give you that joy . . .*

—*But Father, we only want to help . . .*

—*Get out of my room, and don't come back here, not even to get my corpse . . .*

For days, my father lay sick in his bed. His faithful servant, Zachary Kalash, was always by his side. Those days were propitious for us to develop our friendship with Marta. I increasingly regarded her as a mother. Ntunzi increasingly dreamed of her as a woman. My brother became more and more taken by lust: he dreamed of her naked, he would undress her with the urgency of a male, and the Portuguese woman's most intimate items of clothing would fall to the floor of his slumber. What I liked about Marta was her gentleness. She would write, every day, she would be bowed over her papers, writing orderly lines of letters. Just like me, Marta was a foreigner in the world. She wrote memories, I tuned silences.

At night, my brother would boast of the advances he had made on her heart. He was like a general giving details of territories that had been conquered. He claimed he had got a glimpse of her breasts, had caught her at her most intimate moments, had seen her bathing naked. Soon, he would satisfy his hunger in her body. Galvanized by the proximity of that golden moment, my brother would get up in bed and proclaim:

—*Either God exists, or He's about to be born now!*

Such episodes were like a hunter's tale: their telling could only gain the seal of authenticity through a lie. Every one of his stories, however, left me unsettled, hurt, and betrayed. Even though I knew that they were more the product of his fantasies than of facts, Ntunzi's tales filled me with rage. For the first time, there was a woman in my life. And that woman had been sent by the dead Dordalma to watch over what remained of my childhood. Little by little, this foreigner was turning into my mother, in a kind of second round of existence.

* * *

The erotic accounts of my brother may have been the product of his delirium, but three afternoons later I saw Ntunzi lying down with his head on her lap. Such intimacy made me unsure: could the rest of my little brother's romance with the foreign woman be true?

—I'm tired— Ntunzi confessed, drooling over Marta.

The Portuguese woman stroked my brother's forehead and said:

—It's not tiredness. It's sadness. You miss someone. Your illness is called yearning.

It had been so long since our mother had been alive, but she'd never died within my brother's mind. Sometimes, he wanted to cry out in pain, but he didn't have enough life in him for it. The Portuguese woman gave him advice at that point: Ntunzi should go into mourning in order to blunt the vicious spike of nostalgia.

—You've got all these wonderful surroundings to weep in . . .

—What's the use of weeping if I don't have anyone to listen?

—Weep, my darling, and I'll give you my shoulder.

Jealous feelings made me move away, leaving the sad spectacle of Ntunzi lying on top of the intruder with his legs spread. For the first time, I hated my brother. Back in my room, I cried because I felt betrayed by Ntunzi and by Marta.

* * *

To make matters worse, my father recovered. A week after taking to his bed, he stepped out of his room. He sat in his chair on the veranda to catch his breath, as if his illness were no more than a bout of tiredness.

—Do you feel well?— I asked.

—Today, I've woken up alive— he answered.

He ordered Ntunzi to come to him. He wanted to inspect our eyes to see how we were sleeping. Our faces paraded before his fanatical examination.

—You, Ntunzi, woke up late. You didn't even greet the sun.

—I didn't sleep well.

—I know what's depriving you of your sleep.

I closed my eyes, and awaited the expected. I sensed a storm brewing. Either that, or I no longer knew Silvestre Vitalício.

—I'm warning you: if I see you flirting with that Portuguese woman . . .

—But Father, I'm not doing anything . . .

—These things are never being done: they just end up done. Don't come to me afterwards and say I didn't warn you.

I helped the old man back to his resting place. Then, I went to the yard where the Portuguese woman was waiting for me. She wanted me to help her climb a tree. I hesitated. I thought the girl maybe wanted to remember her childhood. But no. She just wanted to check to see whether her cellphone could catch a signal from a higher position. My brother stepped forward and helped her pull herself up through the branches. I realized he was peeping at the white woman's legs. I left, unable to watch this degrading scene.

Later on, as we sat in silence round the table where we had had dinner, old Silvestre suddenly exclaimed:

—Today, everything went backwards for the worse.

—Are you ill again?

—And it's the fault of the pair of you. So now you let that broad climb a tree!?

—What's wrong, Father?

—What's wrong? Have you forgotten that I . . . that I am a tree?

—You can't be serious, Father . . .

—That woman was climbing over me, she was stamping on me with her feet, I had to bear her whole weight on my shoulders . . .

And he fell silent, such was the insult he felt. Only his hands danced around emptily in despair. He got to his feet with difficulty. When I tried to help him, he raised his index finger right in front of our noses.

—Tomorrow, this is going to end.

—What's going to end?

—Tomorrow's the deadline for that floozy to get out of here. Tomorrow's her last day.

* * *

The biggest flash came in the darkness of night: Ntunzi announced that he was going to run away with the foreign woman. He said everything had been arranged. Planned right down to the tiniest detail.

—Marta's taking me to Europe. There are countries there you can enter and leave as well.

That's what makes a place: entering and leaving. That's why we didn't live anywhere at all. I was frozen to the spot at the very thought of my being left alone in the immensity of Jezoosalem.

—I'll go with you— I declared with a whine.

—No, you can't.

—Why can't I?

—They don't allow children your age into Europe.

Then he told me what Uncle said. In those countries, one didn't have to work: wealth was there for everyone, and all you had to do was to fill in the appropriate form.

—I'm going to travel round Europe, arm in arm with the white woman.

—I don't believe you, brother. That girl has gone to your head. Do you remember telling me about your first love? Well, you've gone blind again.

* * *

It wasn't the possibility that Ntunzi might end up leaving. It was the fact that he was leaving with Marta: that's what hurt me most. I couldn't sleep because of it. I peered out at the big house and saw that there was still a lamp shining. I went over to Marta and came straight to the point:

—*I'm very angry with you!*

—*With me?*

—*Why did you choose Ntunzi?*

—*What are you talking about?*

—*I know everything, you're going to run away with my brother. You're going to leave me here.*

Marta put her head back and smiled. She asked me to come over to her. I refused.

—*I'm leaving tomorrow. Don't you want to go for a walk with me?*

—*I want to go away with you once and for all . . . together with Ntunzi.*

—*Ntunzi won't be coming with me. You can be sure of that. Tomorrow, Aproximado arrives with fuel and we'll leave together, just the two of us. Me and your Uncle, no one else.*

—*Do you promise?*

—*I promise.*

The Portuguese woman took my hand and led me to the window. She stood there, looking out at the night as if, for her, all that sky was just one star.

—*Do you see those stars? Do you know what they're called?*

—*The stars don't have names.*

—*They have names, it's just that we don't know them.*

—*My father says that in the city, people gave the stars names. And they did so because they were afraid . . .*

—*Afraid?*

—Afraid because they felt the sky might not belong to them. But I don't believe that. Besides, I know who made the stars.

—It was God, wasn't it?

—No, it was Zachary. With his rifle.

The Portuguese woman smiled. She passed her fingers through my hair and I held her hand up to my face. I had a strong urge to brush my lips over Marta's skin. But then I realized something: I didn't know how to kiss. And this ineptitude hurt me like a prelude to some fatal illness. Marta noticed the shadows falling over my body and said:

—It's late already, go and sleep.

I went back to my room, ready to turn in, when I noticed Silvestre and Ntunzi arguing in the middle of the hall. When I arrived, my old man was decreeing:

—That's the end of the matter!

—Father, I beg of you . . .

—I've made up my mind!

—Please, Father . . .

—I'm your father, whatever I do is for your own good.

—You're not my father.

—What are you saying?

—You're just a monster!

I looked aghast at Silvestre's face: he had more wrinkles than he had face and veins bulged sinisterly along his neck. He opened and closed his mouth more times than his words required. As if speech was too unimportant for such anger. What he wanted to say was beyond any language. I awaited the explosion that always ensued when his blood was up. But no. After a moment, Silvestre calmed down. He even appeared to be conceding to Ntunzi and accepting his arguments. If he surrendered, it would be truly exceptional: my father was as obstinate as a compass needle. And in the end, it was his obstinacy that prevailed. He raised his chin in the pose of a king in a pack of cards, and concluded haughtily:

—*I don't hear anything you say.*

—*Well, this time, you're going to go on not hearing. I'm going to say everything, everything that I've had to keep buttoned up inside me . . .*

—*I can't hear anything*— my father complained, looking at me.

—*You were the opposite of a father. Parents give their children life. You sacrificed our lives for your madness.*

—*Did you want to live in that loathsome world?*

—*I wanted to live, Father. Just live. But it's too late for questions now . . .*

—*I know very well who's put these ideas in your head. But tomorrow, this is going to end . . . once and for all.*

—*Do you know something? For a long time I thought you had killed our mother. But now I know it was the other way round: it was she who killed you.*

—*Shut up or I'll smash your face.*

—*You're dead, Silvestre Vitalício. You stink of rottenness. Even that simpleton Zachary can't stand the smell any more.*

Silvestre Vitalício raised his arm and in a split second brought it down with a smack onto Ntunzi's face. Blood spattered and I threw myself against my father. The struggle was complicated by the Portuguese woman, who appeared from nowhere to intervene. A clumsy dance of bodies and legs circled the room until the three of them fell to the floor in a tangle. They each got to their feet, shook themselves and smoothed their clothes. Marta was the first to speak:

—*Careful now, no one here wants to hit a woman, isn't that so, Mister Mateus Ventura?*

For some time, Silvestre stood there, his movements suspended, arm raised above his head, as if some sudden paralysis had left him comatose. The Portuguese woman went over to him with motherly concern:

—*Mateus . . .*

—*I've told you before not to call me by that name.*

—*One can't spend so much time forgetting. No journey is that long . . .*

We separated, unaware of the mishap that would occur during the night. The tires of Aproximado's truck would be cut to shreds, reduced to the elastic of a catapult. The following morning, the vehicle would wake up paralysed, shoeless on the savannah's scalding earth.

SECOND BATCH
OF PAPERS

On a night of pale moon and geraniums
he'll come, his prodigious mouth and hands,
to play his flute in my garden.
At the onset of my despair
I see but two ways to go:
To become insane or a saint.
I who eschew censure
what isn't natural such as blood and veins
find I'm weeping each day,
my desolate hair,
my skin assailed by indecision.
When he comes, for it's certain he will,
how will I enter the balcony shorn of youth?
The moon, the geraniums and he will be the same
—among all things, only a woman ages.
How will I open the window, if I'm not insane?
How will I close it, if I'm not a saint?

Adélia Prado

I n Lisbon, when I announced that I was going to rescue my husband lost in Africa, my family abandoned its usual indifference. In the heat of the discussion, my father even went as far as to say:

—*There's only one way to describe these ravings, my dear daughter: they're those of a jilted lover!*

I was already weeping, but only noticed my tears at that point. My mother tried to keep the peace. But she reiterated her misgivings: "No one can save a marriage, only love can."

—*And who told you there's no love?*

—*That's even more serious: love is for whoever is beyond salvation.*

The next day, I consulted the newspapers and scanned the classifieds. Before leaving for Africa, I had to make Africa come to me, in what is said to be the most African city in Europe. I would look for Marcelo without having to leave Lisbon. With that conviction, and with the paper opened at the classifieds, my finger paused on Professor Bambo Malunga. Next to the photograph of the soothsayer, his magic skills were listed: "He'll bring back loved ones, find lost friends . . . ." At the end, a note was added: "credit cards accepted." In my case, perhaps it should have been a discredit card.

The following day, I walked down the narrow streets of Amadora carrying a bag full of the stuff stipulated in the ad: "A photo of the person, seven black candles, three white candles, a bottle of wine or spirits."

The man who opened the door was almost a giant. His coloured tunic increased his bulk even more. I was uncertain about addressing him by his title when I introduced myself:

—*I'm the one who phoned you yesterday, professor.*

Bambo was from a part of Africa where the Portuguese hadn't been, but he wasn't put out: "Africans," he said, "are all Bantu, all similar, they use the same subterfuges, the same witchcraft." I pretended I believed him, as I walked past wooden statuettes and printed cloth wall-hangings. The apartment was cluttered and I took care not to tread on the zebra and leopard skins that covered the floor. They might be dead, but one shouldn't step on animals.

Once he'd shown me to a little round stool, the sooth-sayer checked the things I'd brought and then noticed that I'd left something out:

—*There's no item of your husband's clothing here. I told you yesterday on the phone that I needed a piece of his intimate clothing.*

—*Intimate?*— I repeated blankly.

I smiled to myself. All Marcelo's clothes were intimate, they had all brushed against his body, they had all been touched by my enraptured fingers.

—*Come back tomorrow, lady, with all the materials required*— the soothsayer suggested delicately.

Next day, I emptied Marcelo's wardrobe into a holdall and walked through Lisbon carrying the bundle. I didn't get as far as Amadora. Halfway, I stopped by the river and cast the clothes into the water as if I were emptying them onto the floor of the soothsayer's consulting room. I stood there watching them float away, and suddenly, it seemed as if it were Marcelo adrift in the waters of the Tagus.

At that moment, I felt like a witch. First, clothes are an embrace that welcomes us when we are born. Later, we dress the dead as if they were leaving on a journey. Not even Professor Bambo could imagine my magic arts: Marcelo's clothes floated like some prediction of our re-encounter. Somewhere on the continent of Africa, there was a river that would return my sweetheart to me.

* * *

I've just arrived in Africa and the place seems too vast to receive me. I've come to find someone. But ever since I got here, I've done nothing but get lost. Now that I'm settled in the hotel, I realize how tenuous my connection is with this new world: seven numbers scribbled on the back of a photograph. This number is the only bridge leading me to that other bridge I have to cross in order, perhaps, to find Marcelo. There are no friends, there are no acquaintances, there aren't even any strangers. I'm alone, I've never been so alone. My fingers are only too aware of this solitude as they dial the number and then give up. Then, they dial again. Until a voice on the other end answers softly:

—*Speaking?*

The voice left me speechless, I was incapable of saying anything at all. My rival's question was absurd: speaking? I hadn't uttered so much as a word. It would have been more appropriate to ask: not speaking? Seconds later, the voice insisted:

—*It's Noci here? Who is this?*

Noci. So that was her name. Up until then, the other woman was just a motionless face. Now, it was a name and a voice. A shudder returned my voice to me: I revealed everything all at once, as if I could only explain myself by blurting it all out. The woman remained silent for a moment and then, unperturbed, arranged to come to the hotel. An hour later, she introduced herself at the poolside bar. She was young, wore a white dress and matching sandals. Something broke within me. I expected someone of regal bearing. Instead, I was faced with a vulnerable young girl, her fingers trembling as if her cigarette were an unbearable weight.

—*Marcelo left me . . .*

What a strange sensation: my husband's mistress was admitting she'd been abandoned by my husband. Suddenly. I was no longer the betrayed woman. And we two strangers were being transformed into one-time relatives, sharing a common desertion.

—*Marcelo went off with a married woman.*

—*He was involved with a married woman before.*

—*Here?*

—*No, there. It was me. And who is this new woman?*

—*I never found out. But in any case, Marcelo's no longer with her. No one knows where he is.*

She cupped her cigarette ash in her hand. It was the ash falling into her palm in this way that made me understand what she wasn't telling me. I made an excuse to go up to my room. I said I'd only be a minute. But the tears I shed in that brief moment were enough for a lifetime.

I returned, having pulled myself together. Even so, Noci noticed my tortured look.

—*Let's forget Marcelo, forget men . . .*

—*None of them warrants a woman's sadness.*

—*Much less that of two women.*

And so we sat talking about those non-existent things that women know so well how to endow with expressiveness. That woman's loneliness hurt me, for she was hardly more than a girl. She chose me as her confessor, and for some time she complained that she'd suffered for being a white man's lover. In public places, looks condemned her: *she's a whore!* But she told me how her relatives had gone to the other extreme and encouraged her to get out of the country and take advantage of the foreigner. While Noci was talking, I still wondered to myself: if I saw her going into a bar with Marcelo, what would I say, what expressions of outrage would erupt from me? In truth, all I felt for that woman now was sympathy and warmth. For every occasion she had been insulted, I had also been affronted.

—*So what do you do now, Noci?*

To get a job, she had surrendered to the advances of a trader, the owner of a business. His name was Orlando Macara and he was her boss by day and lover by night. At the interview for the position, Orlando arrived late. Limping along like the hand on a clock and looking her up and down with a salacious grin, he said:

—*I don't even need to see your CV. I'll take you on as a receptionist.*

—*Receptionist?*

—*Yes, to give me a reception.*

She'd got a job by walking out on herself. Deep within her, a decision had been reached. She would divide in two just as a fruit separates: her body was the flesh; the seed was her soul. She would surrender her flesh to the appetites of this boss and any others. But her seed would be preserved. At night, after being eaten, sucked and spat out, her body would return to the seed and she would eventually sleep, whole and intact like a fruit. But she could find no rest in her slumber, and this was causing her to slide into despair.

—*Women-friends of mine gossip. But I ask you: now that I'm going with a man of my own race, is it no longer prostitution?*

She wasn't asking for my opinion. Noci had long been sure that it was no use pondering these afflictions. A whore hires out her body. In her case, it was the opposite: her body was hiring her out.

—*I'm fine like I am, believe me.*

The black girl sensed a doubt in my eyes. How can one be happy with a body that is no longer our own? Sex, she said, wasn't done with either our body or our soul. It's done with the body that's under our body. Once again, her fingers trembled, causing her cigarette ash to drop. At that moment, Marcelo's clothes passed before me eyes, floating in the waters of the river. Those clothes had been unbuttoned by those same slender fingers.

—*It's been so long since I made love*— I confessed —*that I can't even remember how to undress a man.*

—*Is that so bad?*

And we laughed, as if we were the oldest of friends. One man's lie had brought us together. What united us was the truth of two lives.

* * *

Orlando Macara, Noci's boss, came to fetch her at the hotel. I was introduced, and from the start, I recognized one thing: the man was the soul of congeniality. He was squat and lame, but exceedingly gracious.

—*How did the two of you meet?*— he asked us.

I had no idea what answer to give. But Noci improvised with surprising ease.

—*We met on the internet.*

And she went on about the advantages and dangers of computers.

Orlando wanted to know why I had come, and what my impressions were. When I mentioned Marcelo, he suddenly seemed to remember something.

—*Have you a photograph of him?*— he asked. I showed him the photo I carry in my wallet. While Orlando looked closely at the details, I addressed Noci:

—*Marcelo came out well in this photo, don't you think?*

—*I've never seen the man before in my life!*— she answered abruptly.

The trader got up and went over to the window with my wallet. I followed his movements somewhat suspiciously, until he suddenly exclaimed:

—*That's him. I took your husband to the reserve.*

—*When was that?*

—*It was some time ago. He wanted to take photos of animals.*

—*So did you leave him there?*

—*Nearly.*

—*What do you mean nearly?*

—I left him just before we got there, near the entrance to the reserve. I don't want to worry you, but he looked ill to me . . .

The illness Marcelo suffered from, I could have replied, was himself. In other words, he was a man beyond remedy.

—So you've never heard any more of Marcelo, whether he came back, or whether he stayed there?

—Stayed there? My dear lady: it's not a place for anyone to stay . . .

* * *

That night, alone in my room, I mulled over the motives that could have led Marcelo to want to travel to the reserve. It can't have been just for the sake of photography. Doubts gnawed away at my sleep, so much so that, first thing in the morning, I summoned the help of Noci's boyfriend. He turned up late, limping so heavily that his lameness didn't seem a defect so much as an apology for his lack of punctuality. Or who knows, maybe it was just out of consideration for the ground he was treading on? Noci was with him. But this time she was so distant and quiet that I hardly recognized the girl from the previous day. I got straight to the point:

—Take me to where you left my husband.

I was waiting for his negative reaction. That it wasn't a place for men, let alone a woman. And a white woman, with all due respect. I pressed him to take me to the reserve.

—But your husband, my dear lady, your husband is no longer there . . .

—I know.

Orlando Macara didn't make things easy. I understood that there was the matter of costs. In the end, we reached an agreement: I would go with him as far as the entrance where he had left Marcelo. After that, Orlando wouldn't have anything more to do with it.

—Why don't you tell her everything, Orlando?

Noci's intervention took me by surprise. She argued on my behalf and revealed that there were relatives of Orlando living in the reserve who would welcome me.

—*Relatives? Funny relatives.*

—*They're a bit strange. But they're good folk.*

—*Don't talk to them, they're all mad.*

Orlando relented and then gave way. Nevertheless, he gave me a whole list of instructions: I should avoid contact with the family living in the encampment. And I should understand the idiosyncrasies of each of the four inhabitants.

—*For example, there, I'm not Orlando.*

—*How do you mean?*

—*I'm Aproximado. That's what they call me there: I'm Uncle Aproximado.*

His condition for driving me there was that I should agree to lie: if they asked me how I had got to the reserve, I was to free Orlando from any responsibility. I'd come on my own.

* * *

Orlando came by my hotel early. I followed his old truck in my car. It was a long journey, the longest I'd ever made in my whole life. The old jalopy was in such a ramshackle condition that the journey would take three days.

I felt like doing something that I would certainly never have the chance to do again: to drive such a decrepit vehicle along such bewildering roads.

—*Orlando, let me drive, just a bit.*

—*You'd better get used to calling me Aproximado.*

He allowed me to drive. But only while we were still in the city. So that's how I found myself driving along narrow suburban thoroughfares. I was rarely able to see the roads, because they surged up before me so full of people and garbage. I guessed where the road was by the two lines of people who walked along on both sides of it. People here

144

don't walk along the sidewalks. They walk along the road as if it were their right.

I wondered to myself: will I be able to drive in this chaos? It was only later that I realized it wasn't me who was doing the driving. It was Marcelo's hands that were driving me, and I had long been blind both to the outside world and to my inner self. I was like an African road: you only realize it exists because of the presence of people walking along it.

I returned the controls to Orlando and went back to my vehicle, now sure of one thing: it made little difference to me whether I drove or was being driven. There was a time when I wanted to travel the world. Now, all I wanted to do was to travel without the world.

* * *

Once we had left the city, the heavens opened: never before had I seen such a deluge. We were forced to stop because the road was unsafe. All of a sudden, I seemed to glimpse Marcelo's clothes being carried along by the torrent of rain-water. And I thought to myself: "The Tagus has burst its banks in tropical soil and my beloved awaits me on some nearby shore."

I thought I knew what it was to rain. But at that moment, I had to reassess the meaning of the verb, and began to fear that I should have hired a boat instead of a motor vehicle. Once the rain had stopped, however, the flood followed: a deluge of light. Intense, all powerful, capable of inducing blindness. Water and light: both billowed up before me indistinctly. Both were boundless, both confirmed my infinitesimal smallness. As if there were thousands of suns, endless sources of light both within and outside of me. Here was my solar side that had never been revealed before. All the colours lost their hues, the entire chromatic spectrum was transformed into a sheet of whiteness.

145

Marcelo always dresses like that, in white. Perhaps he is here, within my field of vision. I know for sure that Marcelo is here, present, within my field of words. I don't just see him because of the reverberation of light, the random occurrence of brightness.

* * *

Farther on, I pass a group of women. They are bathing in the still waters of a pond. Others, a little farther ahead, are washing clothes. I stop the car and walk over. When they see me, they cover themselves with cloth, fastened hurriedly round their waists. Their breasts are withered, hanging lifelessly over their bellies. For sure, Marcelo hadn't allowed himself to be smitten by this type of woman.

I linger for some time, watching them. They laugh as if they can tell my secrets. Could it be that they know of my condition as a betrayed woman? Or does our condition as women unite us, ever betrayed by an unfaithful destiny? Later, these country women take to the road again, carrying cans and bundles on their head. It's only then that I understand how graceful they are capable of being. Their gazelle's step cancels out the weight they carry, their hips swing as if they were ballerinas advancing across an endless stage. They are protagonists of an eternal spectacle, simply because no one ever looks at them. With their can on their head, they cross the frontier between heaven and earth. And I think to myself: that woman isn't carrying water; she's carrying all the rivers within her. It was that spring of water that Marcelo sought to find within his own self.

All of a sudden one of the washerwomen appears to drop some clothes that look very familiar to me. They are shirts of a whiteness that I seem to know. I am gripped by unease: those are Marcelo's clothes. Distressed, I stumble down the slope and the women are frightened by my impetuous approach.

146

They shout out in their language, gather the clothes from the water, and make their escape over the opposite shore.

* * *

We awake early on the second day of the journey. I contemplate the sun rising, and through the dusty haze, it's like a piece of earth that has become separated and is emerging in levitation. Africa is the most sensuous of the continents. I hate having to admit to this cliché. I get out of the car and sit on the back of the truck. This silence isn't like any period of quiet I have ever experienced before. This isn't some absence that we hasten to fill out of fear of emptiness. It's an awakening in our depths. This is what I feel: that I am possessed by silence. Nothing precedes me, I think to myself. And Marcelo is still to be born. I have come to witness his birth.

—*I am the first living creature*— I proclaim out loud, as I reopen my eyes, to the astonishment of Aproximado.

The lights, the shadows, the whole landscape all seem to have been created recently. And even the words: I was the one dressing them, as if they were the children who fill the main squares of small towns on Sunday.

—*See here, Miss Marta. See what I've found*— Aproximado announced, showing me a reel of camera film.

—*Was it my husband's?*

—*Yes, I stopped here with him so that we could have a rest.*

All of a sudden, a shadow was cast over my sense that we were present at the Creation. There is, after all, no beginning. In my life, everything has been in its death throes, on the point of ending. I'm the one who has already been. I've come in search of my husband. If one can call someone a husband who has run off with someone else. This may well be the place where the world is beginning. But it's where I am reaching my end.

* * *

Once again, women. These are other ones, but as far as I am concerned, they are indistinguishable from the previous ones. They cross the road, half-naked. The nakedness of Africans was once a topic of debate between myself and Marcelo. All of a sudden, black bodies emerged onto the market of desire as socially acceptable. Dark-skinned women and men took magazines, newspapers, television, fashion parades, by storm. Their bodies are beautiful, sculpted with grace, equilibrium, eroticism. And I wonder to myself: why did we never notice them before?

How is it that the African woman has changed from being a focus of ethnographic interest to feature on the covers of fashion magazines, in advertisements for cosmetics, or on the catwalks of the world of haute couture? I could see only too well that Marcelo took delight in contemplating these images. A deep anger bubbled inside me. It was clear that the invasion of black sensuality was a sign that values attributed to beauty were becoming less prejudiced. But black female nudity led me to consider my own body. Thinking about how I saw my body, I came to the following conclusion: I didn't know how to be naked. And I realized that what covered me was not so much clothing as shame. It had been like that ever since the time of Eve, ever since the birth of sin. For me, Africa wasn't a continent. It was the fear I had of my own sensuality. One thing seemed obvious to me: if I wanted to win back Marcelo, I would have to allow Africa to emerge within me. I needed to give birth to my own African nudity.

* * *

I take in my surroundings as I crouch down. The ground is criss-crossed by thousands of ants, parading along infinite little tracks. I've heard it said that women from here eat this red

148

sand. When they die, they're eaten by the earth. When they're alive, they devour the very earth that will swallow them up tomorrow.

I pull up my underpants as I get to my feet. I've decided to hold it. My bladder will have to wait for another piece of ground. A ground that isn't being scribbled across by famished insects.

We return to the truck. The road is a serpent undulating on the curve of the horizon. The road is alive, and its huge mouth is devouring me.

The vehicle advances slowly across the savannah, and the track's substance dissolves as the dust cloud rises into the air like a vulture's wings. The dust covers my face, my eyes, my clothes. I'm being turned into earth, buried outside the earth. Could it be that, without realizing it, I'm turning into the African woman who bewitched Marcelo?

MADNESS

When our country is no longer ours to have
Lost to silence and submission
Even the sea's voice becomes exile
and the light around us prison bars

Sophia de Mello Breyner Andresen

—*What are you doing here?*

The papers plummeted to the floor. I thought their fall would be a gradual, fluttering descent. On the contrary, they collapsed in one solid sheaf and the noise they made caused the crickets around the house to fall silent.

—*Were you reading my letters?*

—*I don't know how to read, Miss Marta.*

—*So what were you doing with those papers in your hand?*

—*It's just that I'd never seen . . .*

—*Never seen what?*

—*Papers.*

Marta bent down to pick up the sheets. She checked them one by one, as if each contained some incalculable fortune.

—*My father's yelling over at the camp. I think I'd better go.*

* * *

The slashed tires of the Portuguese woman's car had driven my father completely mad. On the veranda, the dishevelled Silvestre wailed:

—*I'm surrounded by traitors and cowards.*

His list of deserters was a long one: his eldest son didn't respect him, his brother-in-law had joined the ones from Over There; someone had been delving around in his money box; and even Zachary Kalash was falling into disobedient ways.

—*You're the only one left, my son, you're the only one who hasn't abandoned me yet.*

He took a step forward to touch me, but I avoided him, pretending to tie my shoes, and that's how I stayed, my head bowed, until he moved off to his usual place of rest. My eyes didn't leave the ground, for I knew only too well that he would read my seditious thoughts.

—*Come here, Mwanito. I feel a need for a bit of silence.*

Seated in his armchair, he closed his eyes and let his arms drop as if they were no longer his. I almost felt sorry for Silvestre. On the other hand, I could never forget that those same arms had repeatedly beaten my poor brother. And, who knows, those arms might have strangled Dordalma, my beloved mother.

—*I'm not feeling anything, Mwanito, what's happening?*

Silence is a crossing. You need baggage to brave that journey. At that moment, Silvestre was drained. And I was brimming with bitterness and suspicion. How could I conjure up a silence with so much buzzing around in my head? I got up hurriedly, bowed my head respectfully as I passed the armchair, and moved away.

—*Don't leave me, my son, I've never felt so much despair before . . . Mwanito, come back.*

I didn't go back. I stayed in the corner, hidden by the adjoining wall. I listened to the rattling of his chest. The old man seemed at the point of sobbing. But suddenly, what followed left me thunderstruck: my father was humming a tune! For the first time in my eleven years of life, I heard my old man sing. It was a sad piece and his voice was like a tiny trickle of water made from morning mist. I drew my knees up close to me and hugged them with my arms: my father was singing and his voice was accomplishing the divine mission of chasing away the dark clouds.

I concentrated, listening with my whole body, as if I knew that this was the first and last time I would hear Vitalício in song.

—*I like what I'm hearing, brother.*

I almost leapt with fright at Aproximado's arrival. My father got an even greater fright, ashamed at having been caught red-handed singing his old favourites.

—*It just came out, without my being aware.*

—*I often remember the choir of our church, and you, Silvestre, were the maestro, you were so good at it . . .*

—*I'm going to confess something to you, brother. There's nothing I miss more.*

More than people, more than love and friends. It was the absence of music he found hardest. In the middle of the night, he said, under his sheets and blankets, he sang almost imperceptibly. Then the other voices would come to him, pinpointed with such clarity that only God could hear them.

—*That's why I don't allow the kids to come near my room at night.*

—*So, my dear old Silvestre, you were flouting the rules after all . . .*

There were so many times, he admitted at that moment, so many times when he felt like asking Aproximado to bring him his old accordion from the city. All this, Silvestre

Vitalício confessed, while his hands shook so much, that the other became concerned:

—Are you all right, brother?

Silvestre got to his feet to calm his nerves. He pushed his shoulders back, tightened his belt, coughed and declared:

—I'm fine, yes, it was just a momentary thing.

—That's just as well, my dear Brother-in-law, because I've come to talk to you about something that certainly isn't momentary.

—The way you put it, it can't be something good . . .

—As I already told you, I've been re-appointed to the Department for Fauna, but I now have new responsibilities . . .

My father took his cigarette tin out of his pocket and started the long ritual of rolling tobacco. He looked up at the visitor once again:

—You're where suits you best, Aproximado, working in a department for animals . . .

—And it's in this new role that I've come to give you notice of something you're not going to like. My dear Silvestre, you've got to leave here.

—What do you mean leave here?

—A development project has been agreed upon for this area. The reserve has been privatized.

—I can't speak this language. Explain it more clearly.

—The Department for Fauna has given this concession to foreign private investors. You're going to have to leave.

—You must be joking. These private foreigners should come and talk to me when they get here.

—You're going to have to leave before that.

—How funny: I was waiting for God to come to Jezoosalem. But in the end, it's a bunch of private foreigners that are coming.

—That's the way of the world . . .

—Who knows, maybe the private foreigners are the new gods?

—Who knows?

—It's strange how people change.

Silvestre reviewed developments so far: at first, Aproximado was almost his brother, all brother-in-lawish, they were all one family, full of mutual help and kindness. Then, this help began to be paid for and his comings and goings had become a business, with cash demanded up front. More recently, Aproximado had turned up with the jargon of a government functionary, to tell him that the State wanted him out of there. Now, there he was again, with a story about money, declaring that some nameless and faceless foreigners were the new owners.

—Don't forget, Brother-in-law, there's a world out there. And that world has changed. It's globalization . . .

—And what if I don't leave? Will they force me out?

—No, certainly not. International donors are sensitive to human rights. There's a resettlement plan for the local communities.

—So now I'm a local community?

—It's much better like that, my dear Brother-in-law. It's much better than being Silvestre Vitalício.

—In that case, if I'm a community, you're no longer my Brother-in-law.

Silvestre rammed his point home, his finger erect, his voice abrupt: that his ex-brother-in-law, now state official, should be left in no doubt that only cattle can be re-settled. That he, Silvestre Vitalício, once known as Mateus Ventura, would die right there, next to the River Kokwana that he himself had baptized.

—Do you understand, Mister Official? And it's my two sons here who'll bury me . . .

—Your sons? Your sons have decided they're going with me. You're going to be left on your own.

—Zachary won't leave me . . .

—I've spoken to Zachary, he's also reached the end.

My old man raised his head, his gaze blank, brooding. I knew: he was delving into himself to find the ingredients of patience.

—*Is that all the news you have, Brother-in-law?*

—*I have no more. Now, I'm going.*

—*Before you go, my friend, tell me something: what's your name?*

—*What are you playing at, Silvestre?*

—*I'm going to show you something, my dear stranger. Don't be offended if that's what I call you, I've always preferred strangers to friends . . .*

While he was speaking, he got up, and thrusting his hands deep into his pockets, he pulled out a bundle of notes, which he placed in a pile at his feet.

—*I've always preferred friends to relatives. You now have the advantage of being a stranger.*

He bent down and lit a match with his right hand, cupping it with his left.

—*What are you doing, Silvestre? Are you crazy?*

—*I'm smoking your money.*

—*That money, Silvestre, is to pay me for your goods . . .*

—*It was.*

Incredulity etched into his face, Aproximado walked off and almost stumbled over me as he turned the corner. I remained motionless, peering at the veranda. From where I was I could see my old man sink back into his old armchair, sighing noisily and uttering the most unexpected words:

—*Not long now, my little Alma. Not long now.*

My skin was covered in goosebumps when I stalked off furtively, like a shadow among the bushes. Once I was at a safe distance, I ran as fast as I could.

* * *

—*Who are you running from, Mwanito?*

Zachary was sitting by the door of the ammunition store, his hand gripping his pistol as if he had just fired it.

I stopped immediately and sat down next to the soldier. I sensed that he wanted to tell me something. But he sat there for some time without saying a word, while he used the barrel of his gun to make drawings in the sand. I began to pay attention to the scribbling carved in the ground and suddenly, it dawned on me that Zachary was writing. And I was struck by the letters he had written: Dordalma.

—*My mother?*

—*Don't forget, kid: you can't read. How did you do it? Did you guess?*

I realized it was too late: Kalash was a hunter and I had stepped on the trap he had set.

—*And I know more, kid. I know where you've hidden the papers you've been writing on.*

It was now obvious that he would go and tell his boss and my father, Silvestre Vitalício. It wouldn't be long before Ntunzi and I would both join the excommunicated.

—*Have no fear. I've also lied because of some words and a few papers.*

He erased my mother's name with the sole of his foot. The grains of sand swallowed up the letters, one by one, as if the earth were once again devouring Dordalma. Then Zachary told me what had happened to him in his days as a commando in the colonial army. The mail would arrive and he was the only one never to get a letter. Zachary was always excluded, making him feel the burden of race: not the race determined by skin colour, but the race of those who are always denied joy.

—*No woman ever wrote to me. For me, Jezoosalem started even before I got here . . .*

Half a dozen Portuguese soldiers, none of whom could read, had chosen him to decipher the letters they got from

Portugal. His moment had come. He would sit on the top bunk in their sleeping quarters, while the whites would contemplate him as if he were some powerful prophet.

But this passing cause for vanity couldn't match the ecstasy of those receiving the letters. Zachary's envy knew no bounds. From the other side of the world came women, romance, comfort. Even the name of the letters made him feel jealous: "aerogramme." For him, it sounded almost like the name of a bird. Then, he got the idea of passing himself off as a Portuguese. And that was how Zachary Kalash, through an unexpected switch of identity, got himself a godmother of war.

—*This is her, look. Maria Eduarda, Dadinha . . .*

He showed me a photo of a light-skinned woman, her hair swept over her eyes, and wearing large earrings. I smiled to myself: my warless godmother, my Marta, was certainly much whiter than that sad-eyed woman. Zachary didn't notice how remote I had become for a moment. The soldier put the photograph back in his pocket while he explained that he never allowed himself to be separated from that paper talisman.

—*It's protection against bullets.*

Zachary and his godmother had corresponded for months. When the war was over the soldier confessed that he had faked his identity. She replied immediately: she had also given a false name, age, and place. Maria Eduarda wasn't a twenty-one year old girl, the profile of those required to sustain the morale of young men through their letters.

—*Each one of us was a lie, but the two of us together, we were true. Do you understand, Mwanito?*

* * *

The following morning, Jezoosalem was a hive of activity. Once again, we had been summoned to the square by Silvestre. A rather downhearted and unconvinced Zachary was the one who communicated the order and made us line up next to the crucifix. We were the usual number. But this time, there was a woman. This woman, standing straight-backed beside me, seemed both astonished and fearful. On her chest, her camera rivalled the rifle that Kalash wore across his shoulder.

—*When is he going to appear?*— Marta asked, with the anxiousness of a spectator.

I didn't get as far as answering. For we heard strange sounds, similar to a flock of frightened partridges. Then Silvestre made his spectacular appearance: turning himself into a motor vehicle while emitting the intermittent wailing of sirens. His theatre sent a simple message: a person of authority was arriving. He pretended the door of the imaginary car was being opened. He climbed, haughtily, onto a non-existent podium and declared:

—*Ladies and Gentlemen. I have called this meeting for reasons of the utmost gravity. I have received alarming reports from our Security and Defence Forces.*

We stood there, speechless and expectant. Next to me, Marta looked agog and murmured: "Fantastic, he's a hell of an actor!" The orator's quizzical gaze swept slowly over those present until it came to rest on my brother. It wasn't long before an accusing arm was raised:

—*You there, young citizen!*

—Me? Ntunzi asked, agape.

—*I'm told you sleep there, in her house, the Portuguese woman's house.*

—*It's not true.*

—*Have you fucked the whore yet?*

—*What are you saying, Father?*

—*Don't call me Father . . .*

His uncontrolled shriek left us baffled. I stared, aghast, at his expression: the lines on his face overspilled his frown and veins stood out from his neck malevolently. His mouth was opening and closing more than his words required. For the insane, words are always in vain. Whatever it was he wanted to say was beyond any language. Ntunzi's alarmed eyes latched onto mine, seeking some meaning for what we were hearing.

—*From now on, there'll be no more talk of "Father this, Father that." From today, I am the Authority. Or better still, I am the President.*

He pretended he was stepping down from the podium, and then walked up the line, inspecting each one of us closely. When he got to the Portuguese woman, he excused himself and took her camera from her.

—*Confiscated. It will be returned to you upon your departure from this territory, my dear lady. Without the film, of course. I shall pass it over to my Minister of the Interior here.*

Whereupon, he handed the machine to Zachary. The Portuguese woman made as if to protest. But Aproximado's look convinced her not to do anything. Silvestre returned to the podium, drank from a glass of water, and cleared his throat before continuing:

—*Jezoosalem is a young, independent nation and I am the President. I am the President of the Nation.*

And as he refined his terms, he became even more puffed up with pride at his own titles:

—*In fact, as my name, Vitalício, suggests, I am President for Life . . .*

His bulging eyes alighted on me. But instead of looking at him, I focused on the fly crawling across his beard. As far as I was concerned, it was the same fly as ever, following the same route: it crossed his left cheek and ascended in the direction of his forehead awaiting the brisk slap that would send it spinning into the air. My father had indeed been transformed. Previously, I used to fear losing my father. Now, I couldn't wait to be an orphan.

—*It is a pity that our youth, lifeblood of the nation, should be so depraved, we who placed such hopes . . .*

Once again, I sought out Ntunzi's gaze, hoping for some look of solidarity and understanding. But unlike Marta, my brother seemed terrified. Zachary and Aproximado exuded concern. Their apprehension reinforced my own when the new Silvestre announced his final decision:

—*For reasons of security, an obligatory curfew will be imposed throughout the nation.*

And martial law would be imposed in response to that which he designated, looking hard at Marta, as "interference by colonial powers." Everything would be subject to his direct presidential supervision. And all acts would be executed with the help of his right-hand man, Minister Zachary Kalash.

As he walked off, flanked by a glorious mirage of light, he turned to us with a concluding statement:

—*I have spoken . . .*

ORDERS TO KILL

I rose from my corpse, I went
in search of who I am. Pilgrim of myself,
I have gone to her, she who sleeps in a country
blown by the wind.

Alejandra Pizarnik

The truth is sad when it is only one. Sadder still when its ugliness doesn't have, like Zachary's aerogrammes, the remedy of a lie. At that particular moment in Jezoosalem, the truth was that our father had gone mad. And it wasn't the madness of benevolence and redemption. It was a demon that had taken up residence within him.

—*I'll talk to him*— Marta said, noting the general concern.

Ntunzi didn't think it a good idea. Aproximado, on the other hand, encouraged her to visit the old ranter in his lair. I would accompany the Portuguese woman to make sure that the situation didn't get out of hand.

The moment we entered the half-light of the room, we were brought to a halt by Silvestre's gruff voice:

—*Did you request an audience?*

—*I did. I spoke to the Minister, Zachary.*

Marta was playing her part to an extent that Silvestre couldn't have anticipated. My father's expression was tinged with surprise and suspicion. The foreign woman got to the point without more ado:

—*I've come to tell you that I am going to comply with your instructions, Your Excellency.*

—*You're going to leave Jezoosalem? How?*

—*I'll walk the twenty kilometres to the entrance gate. After that, I'll find someone to help me on the road.*

—*In that case, you have immediate authorization.*

—*The problem is the track within the reserve. It's not safe. I would ask your Minister for the Army to arrange for an escort as far as the gate.*

—*I don't know, I'll think about it. To be honest, I wouldn't want to leave you alone with Zachary.*

—*Why?*

—*I no longer trust him.*

After a pause, he added:

—*I don't trust anyone.*

The Portuguese woman approached him, almost maternally. It looked as if her hand was going to touch our old man's shoulder, but then the visitor thought better.

—*Dearest Silvestre, you know only too well what is needed here.*

—*Nothing is needed here. Nor anyone for that matter.*

—*What's missing here is a farewell.*

—*Yes, your farewell.*

—*You never bade farewell to your late wife. That's what is tormenting you, that lack of proper mourning doesn't bring you any peace.*

—*I do not authorize you to talk about such matters, I am the President of Jezoosalem, and I don't need advice coming from Europe.*

—But I learnt this here, with you, in Africa. Dordalma needs to die in peace, to die definitively.

—Leave the Presidential Palace before my fury prevents me from being responsible for my actions.

I took the Portuguese woman by the hand and hurried her from the room, I knew my father's limits, even when he was in his normal state. In these circumstances, his madness was making him still more unpredictable. Before we left, Marta took a step back and once again confronted the irate Silvestre.

—Just tell me one thing. She was leaving, wasn't she?

—What do you mean?

—On the bus, Dordalma. She was running away from home . . .

—Who told you?

—I know, I'm a woman.

* * *

—You can prime your rifle, my dear Zachary.

—But, Silvestre, is it to kill someone?

—To kill, and to kill stone dead.

Zachary should feel happy to receive such a major responsibility. Killing wild animals wasn't a task worthy of a career soldier. It was when God created Man that he earned his certificate. Wild animals aren't yet proper living creatures. It's Man who can be patented. Only by tearing out the last page of God's book can he defy divine power.

One couldn't say what the soldier's feelings were when he was given the mission to kill the Portuguese woman. To me, he looked impassive. And that's how Zachary left, rifle over his shoulder, his expression impenetrable, his step silent, before my stupefied state. I looked at my father sitting there like a king on his new throne. There was no point in my throwing myself at his feet to appeal for clemency. It was irreversible: Marta, my recent mother, was going to be killed without my being able to do anything about it. Where could Ntunzi be? I ran across the room, the kitchen, the hall. There was no sign of my brother. And Uncle Aproximado hadn't yet arrived from the other side of the world. I threw myself to the ground, empty and defeated, awaiting the inevitable shot. Would I know how to be an orphan all over again?

But nothing happened. The soldier couldn't have gone far, for a few minutes later he was back, his shadow filling the doorway of our house.

—*What's happened?*— my old man asked.

—*I couldn't.*

—*Nonsense. Go back there and do what I told you to do.*

—*I can't.*

—*Have you stopped being a soldier?*

—*I've stopped being Zachary Kalash.*

—*Nonsense*— insisted my father. —*The order I gave you . . .*

—*Don't get angry, Silvestre, but not even God could give me that order.*

—*Get out of here, Zachary Kalash. Go out the back, and you two as well, you're no longer my sons.*

The only creature that merited his affection was Jezebel. And he, Silvestre Vitalício, was going to send us to the corral. In exchange, his sweetheart would come and live inside the house. His decision was final and irrevocable.

* * *

I accompanied Zachary to the ammunition store, while Ntunzi went to look for the foreign woman. While we were walking along, the soldier bemoaned his situation the whole way. He declared his regrets, as if he were asking us for absolution:

—*I helped to kill your childhood.*

And he repeated:

—*Half of what I did was wrong; and the rest was a lie.*

The only thing he had left of any value and integrity was his marksmanship. The sure way he saved the animals he hunted from being killed.

When we were sitting in his doorway, we asked him to forget his rancour. The man made no reply. He pulled up his trousers and showed us his legs:

—*See? They can no longer contain the bullets.*

And a bullet fell to the ground just like that.

—*They're talking to me.*

—*Who?*

—*The bullets. They're telling me the war's over and not coming back.*

—*Wasn't it you who said that wars never end?*

—*Who knows? Maybe what went on in our country wasn't even a war*— Zachary said, as if he were lamenting the fact.

—*How could I know? I've always lived here, far from everything . . .*

—*That's what I wanted too, to live far from everything, far from wars. But now, I'm leaving.*

With Peace declared Over There, what was holding him back here? Even though I understood, I found it hard to accept his reasons.

—*Why did you never leave before?*

—*Because of Silvestre.*

—*You always obeyed him like a son.*

—*It was even worse*— he said.

—*I'm going to tell you a story, something that really happened to me . . .*

It happened in the Colonial War, while on a patrol up in the North, near the frontier. The Portuguese military column with which Zachary was travelling was late getting back to its base, and had to spend the night by the river. They were taking with them women and children who had been captured in a village. In the middle of the night, a child began to cry. The officer commanding the platoon summoned Scrap and told him:

—*You're going to have to take care of that baby.*

—*Don't tell me to do that, please.*

—*The kid won't keep quiet.*

—*It must be sick.*

—*We can't take any risks.*

—*I beg of you, don't tell me to do it.*

—*Don't you know what an order is? Or do you want me to speak to you in that lousy useless language of yours?*

And the officer turned his back.

* * *

Kalash's tale was interrupted by the arrival of Ntunzi. He hadn't found the Portuguese woman. On the other hand, he said he had heard the engine of Aproximado's truck. Perhaps that was the vehicle that was going to take Marta to her destination.

I looked at Zachary's sad face. I waited for him to finish his interrupted story. But the soldier seemed to have forgotten the tale.

—*So did you obey him, Zaca?*

—*What?*

—*Did you obey the officer's order?*

No, he hadn't obeyed the order. He led the child away, and asked a family in the vicinity to take him in. Every so often, he would drop by and give them some money and combat rations.

—*I was the one who gave that kid a name.*

* * *

Zaca stopped at this point. He got up, and the bullets fell to the ground, tinkling on the cement.

—*You can keep them, a souvenir of me . . .*

He slammed the door of his room and left us to ruminate on the possible outcomes of that episode from the war. There was a message in his story and I wanted Ntunzi to help me decipher its hidden meaning. But my brother was in a hurry and ran off down the path.

—*Come on, little brother*— he urged me.

I ran after him. Ntunzi must surely be in a hurry to know what our uncle had brought from the city this time. But that wasn't the reason for his anxiety. We circled the house and saw Aproximado and Silvestre talking in the living room by the light of an oil lamp. Ntunzi immediately walked round the truck, opened the door and jumped up into the driver's seat. He spoke as quietly as he could as he called me over to the window:

—*The keys are here! Mwanito, get out of the way so you don't get run over.*

I didn't wait: in a flash, I was in the passenger seat, urging him to get going. We would escape, the two of us, throwing up dust along unknown highways until we made our triumphal entrance into the city.

—*Do you know how to drive, Ntunzi?*

The question was totally absurd. And the moment he turned the key in the ignition, my father and uncle came through the door, with a look of astonishment on their faces. The truck gave a lurch, Ntunzi pressed his foot down hard on the accelerator and we were catapulted forward into the darkness. The headlights blinded us more than they lit up the road. The truck careered past the haunted house and we saw Marta open the door and dash after us.

—*Keep your eyes on the road, Ntunzi*— I implored.

My words were in vain. Ntunzi couldn't take his eyes off the rearview mirror. That's when we crashed into it. We were aware of a loud noise, as if the world had been split in half. We'd just obliterated the crucifix in the middle of the little square. The sign welcoming God was sent flying through the air and fell, miraculously, at Marta's feet. The vehicle slowed down but didn't stall. On the contrary, the old truck, like some raging buffalo, once again began to kick up dust and regain speed. Ntunzi got as far as shouting:

—*The brake, the fucking brake . . .*

A violent collision followed almost immediately. A baobab took the old rattletrap in its arms, as if nature had swallowed up all the machinery in the world. A cloud of smoke enveloped us. The first person on the scene was the Portuguese woman. It was she who helped us out of the wrecked vehicle. My father had remained behind, next to the crushed altar, and was shouting:

—*It would be better if you'd died, boys. What you've done here, to this sacred monument, is an offence against God . . .*

Overwhelmed, Aproximado paid us no attention: he inspected the damage to the chassis, opened the hood, peered in at its inner workings and shook his head:

—*No one's ever going to leave here now.*

* * *

We returned to the camp after leaving Marta at the big house. My father still paused for a moment beside the destroyed altar piece. We walked along in silence, silence even dripped from my brother's lowered eyes. Suddenly our old man emerged from the darkness and muscling his way past us, declared:

—*I'm going to kill her!*

He entered the house and, seconds later, re-emerged carrying an old shotgun.

—*I'm going to kill her myself.*

The soldier Kalash intervened, blocking our father's path. A crooked smile deformed Silvestre's face and voice:

—*What's this, Zachary?*

—*I'm not letting you pass, Silvestre.*

—*You, Zachary . . . Ah! Of course, you've stopped being Zachary . . . I'll correct myself, then: you, Ernie Scrap, my old son-of-a-bitch, you have betrayed me . . .*

He took a step towards Kalash, prodded his shoulder with his gun and pushed him up against the wall:

—*Remember that shot in the shoulder?*

We were baffled: suddenly, a look of panic dominated the soldier's face. He tried to slip away, but the barrel of the gun pinned him in place.

—*Remember, don't you?*

A trickle of blood appeared: his old wound had re-opened. The soldier had been hit again by the bulllet of old. Silence reigned, and then Aproximado attempted to intervene:

—*For the love of God, Silvestre!*

—*Shut your trap, you useless cripple . . .*

I'll never quite believe what happened next, no matter how often I recall it. With astonishing serenity, my brother Ntunzi stepped forward and asserted:

—*Give me the gun, Father. I'll go.*

—*You?*

—*Give me the gun, I'll kill the Portuguese woman.*

—*You?*

—*Didn't you send me to learn how to kill, Father? Well, I'm going to kill.*

Silvestre circled his son, venting surprise, oozing suspicion.

—*Zachary!*

—*Yes, Silvestre?*

—*Go with him. I want a report . . .*

—*Don't involve Ernie in this, Father. I'll go alone.*

With a dreamlike slowness, my father handed the gun to his son. Ntunzi vanished into the dark. We listened to his determined footsteps fade away, swallowed by the sand. After a time, we heard a shot. My whole body was shaken by weeping. Silvestre's threat was immediate:

—*Any more tears, and I'll kick you to pieces.*

Sobs tumbled from my breast, and my arms quivered as if my inner being were being wracked by some deep schism.

—*Be quiet!*

—*I ca . . . I can't.*

—*Stand up straight and sing!*

I stood to attention, in readiness. But my breast was still overflowing, heaving.

—*Sing!*

—*But Father, sing what?*

—*Sing the national anthem, then!*

—*I'm sorry, Father, but . . . what nation's anthem?*

Silvestre Vitalício looked at me, shocked at my question. His chin trembled, stunned by the simple logic of what I had asked. My only nation was the one we had left far behind, the house where I was born. And that nation's flag was blind, deaf and mute.

* * *

Ntunzi's deranged eyes squinted at the room and his voice was unrecognizable when he blustered his confession:

—*Tonight it was the broad's turn. Tomorrow, I'm going to kill him.*

—*Ntunzi, please, put the gun down.*

But he fell asleep hugging it to him. That night I couldn't sleep, beset by fear. I peered out at the haunted house. There was no sign of a lamp. The job had been done. I looked up at the sky to distract myself, my fear turning into panic. Up in the heavens there were no fixed heavenly bodies: all the stars were cascading, all the lights incandescent. On the darkened wall where Ntunzi had recorded the days passing, all the stars had fallen. Now, no stars shone in Jezoosalem, either down below or in the sky above.

I closed the window abruptly. Our world was crumbling away like a dry clod of earth.

* * *

It was already late afternoon and none of us had been out of the house. A sultriness suddenly made itself felt. First came the smell: the smell of a dead body, eaten up by the heat, chewed over by the sun. My father sent me out to see. Could it be the Portuguese woman who was beginning to decompose?

—*Is she already smelling, so soon? Zachary, go out and bury the Portagee woman.*

She shouldn't be left to rot thereabouts, attracting the big cats. Zachary went out and I overcame my lethargy and followed him. I was going to come face to face with death, stab myself with its cruel truth. Vultures circling in the sky led us out to the back. Ntunzi had dragged the body quite near to our house. And there we saw the corpse surrounded by voracious birds, squabbling and avoiding each other, hopping ridiculously away from their mutually traded ferocities. When Zachary got there, the flock gave way, and I saw the sight with my own eyes: the donkey, Jezebel, my old man's faithful lover, lay torn to pieces by the vultures.

BOOK THREE

REVELATIONS
AND RETURNS

The God I speak of
Is not a God of embraces.
He is mute. Alone. Aware
of Man's greatness
(and his baseness too)
And over time He ponders
The being that was thus created.
[...]

Hilda Hilst

LEAVE-TAKING

In honour of your absence
I avidly built a great white house
And all along its walls I wept for you

Sophia de Mello Breyner Andresen

The image of the donkey's mangled body drained my sleep all night long. I couldn't imagine how much blood a furry creature can contain. It was as if the jenny had turned into a river of red waters, pumped out by a heart that was larger than the earth itself.

Next day, my father went to bury Jezebel alone. First thing in the morning, his spade was already busy in his hands. We offered our help from afar.

—*I don't want anyone here*— he yelled.

Nor did we want to get too near. Silvestre's look was vengeful. Zachary walked round our house, his rifle at the ready, watching my father.

—*No one go near him*— the soldier warned.

He spoke as if about a rabid dog. Despite the warning, I decided to approach the place where Silvestre was guarding the dead donkey. Night had fallen and there by the grave he remained, toe to spade. I advanced, stepping lightly out of respect for his vigil, and coughed quietly before asking:

—*Aren't you coming in to sleep, Father?*

—*I'm staying right here.*

—*All night?*

He nodded. I sat down carefully, some way off. I remained silent, knowing that there would be no more words spoken. But conscious too that no silence could fill that moment or any other moment ever again. In the distance, we could hear Aproximado hammering on metal as he repaired the damaged vehicle. Ntunzi was helping Uncle and a beam of torchlight helped them both.

My father was the picture of grief. Defeated, solitary, disbelieving in everything and everyone. Without raising his head, he murmured:

—*Son, give me your hand.*

I thought I hadn't heard him properly. I remained impassive, keeping my astonishment to myself, until once again Silvestre implored:

—*Don't leave me here all alone.*

I lay down and fell asleep to the rhythm of the hammering coming from the improvised workshop. For me, that episode marked the end of Jezoosalem. Maybe that was why my sleep was disturbed by a nightmare. I was assailed by a vision that kept returning, no matter how hard I tried to chase it away: next to me, between myself and my father, a huge snake had settled itself. It was inert, as if asleep, and my old man, lying next to it, contemplated it with a look of fascination.

—*Come here, son, come and get yourself bitten.*

A snake isn't an animal: it's a muscle with teeth, a legless centipede with a stomach in the middle of its neck. How could Silvestre Vitalício be so enamoured with such a lowly animal?

—*Get bitten?*

—I've already been stung.

—I don't believe you, Father.

—See how swollen my hand is, how its colour has changed. My hand, my dear Mwanito, already belongs to the race of the dead.

It was a hand without an arm, without veins, without nerves. A piece of body without family or familiarity. Silvestre added:

—I'm like that hand.

He'd been born without wishing to be, he'd lived without desires, and he was dying without warning or alarm.

The snake decided to abandon its immobility and little by little began to coil itself sensually around me. I resisted by trying to back away slowly.

—Don't do that, Mwanito.

And he explained: that snake was none other than Time. For years, he had resisted the snake's incursions. On this night, he had surrendered, given up.

—Can't you hear the bells?

It was the hammering on the metal panels of the truck. But I didn't disabuse him. I had another concern: the snake was staring at me, but couldn't decide whether to sink its fangs into me. It seemed hypnotized, unable to act in accordance with its own nature.

—It doesn't even need to bite— Silvestre explained. —Its poison is passed on through its eyes.

That's what had happened to him: while the snake had fixed his eyes with its own, his entire past had come to his mouth. The snake didn't even need to bite him. The poison coursed through his insides in anticipation and Time began to fester inside his body. When, eventually, its slender fangs plunged into him, Silvestre could no longer see the venomous creature: it was no more than a memory, nebulous and dense, slipping away between the dew and the stones. And that was how his remaining memories paraded past him, slithering, viscous like snakes. Sluggish, almost timeless, like the heavy flow of rivers.

—*Time is a poison, Mwanito. The more I remember, the less alive I become.*

—*Do you remember my mother, Father?*

—*I didn't kill Dordalma. I swear, my son.*

—*I believe you, Father.*

—*It was she alone who killed herself.*

People believe they commit suicide. And it's never like that. Dordalma, poor soul, didn't know. She was still convinced that someone could cancel their existence. When it comes to it, there's only one true suicide: to stop having a name, to lose any awareness of oneself and of others. To be beyond the reach of words and the memories of others.

—*I killed myself far more than Dordalma ever did.*

He, Silvestre Vitalício, had certainly committed suicide. Even before reaching death, he had put an end to his life. He swept places aside, banished the living from himself, erased time. My father had even stolen names from the dead. The living aren't, after all, mere buriers of bones: they are, before anything else, shepherds of the deceased. There isn't an ancestor who's not certain that, on the other side of light, there's always someone to rouse him. In my father's case, that wasn't so. Time had never happened to him. The world was beginning within itself, humanity was ending within it, without precedent or antecedent.

—*Father, is that snake also going to open the doors of the past to me?*

Silvestre didn't answer. Instead, he crawled forward like a hunter. Even a sleepwalker has the honour-bound duty to kill a deadly snake. Was it such a command that caused my father to rush after the snake and club it to death?

Can a snake lie down? Well that one melted away like a shadow, forever expired. Old Silvestre bemoaned his sudden gesture that had worn his joints away:

—*My bones have died . . .*

Vitalício lamented the extinction of his own skeleton. While in my case, my bones were the only living part of me.

* * *

The following morning, they came and woke me up. I had fallen asleep exhausted, some metres from Jezebel's grave. Next to me, Silvestre Vitalício was still asleep, all curled up. When I got to my feet, my Uncle was already prodding his brother-in-law with the tip of his foot. Silvestre's body rolled over as if devoid of life. How could he have sunken into such a deep sleep? Why was there thick, white froth seeping from his mouth? The answer wasn't late in coming: there were two threads of blood from a small wound on his arm.

—*He's been bitten! Silvestre has been bitten!*

Alarmed, Uncle called for Zachary and Ntunzi. The soldier rushed over with a knife and in a flash cut my father's arm and then, leaning over him like a vampire, sucked the bloody wound.

—*Don't do that!* I responded heatedly. —*Don't do anything, it was all a dream!*

They looked at me, puzzled, and Zachary detected some sort of mental torpor in my words that led him to inspect me in search of the pinprick that might explain my confused state. Finding nothing, they carried Silvestre away in a state of semi-consciousness. In Zachary's arms, my father looked like a child, even younger than I was. Words tumbled from his mouth like remnants of food, grains of rice lodged in an old man's gums.

—Dordalma, Dordalma, not even God is enough, nor are you going . . .

* * *

They left me alone with Silvestre, while they prepared for the emergency.

—So here I am— he sighed.

And he slowly passed his hands up and down in his arms to show the extent of his disintegration, viscous as if he were returning to clay rather than to dust.

—Father, go and wait quietly in the shade.

—I'm going to die, Mwanito. I'll have too much shade before long.

—Don't say that, Father. You're vaccinated.

—Let me ask you, my son: wouldn't you like to die with me?

It's solitude that we most fear in death, he continued. Solitude, no more than solitude. Silvestre Vitalício's expression was vague and vacant. I got a sudden fright: my father no longer had a face. All he had were his eyes, pools without a shore, into which our anguished moments rushed headlong.

—My blood is what makes your blood flow, did you know that?

Those words had the weight of a sentence. His life, as Ntunzi used to say, had never allowed me to live. The strange thing was that he seemed to be dying within his own death.

—Look— he said, holding out his hand. *—They're two almost invisible holes. And yet, a whole life is draining out through them.*

* * *

Could Silvestre Vitalício be dying? His face didn't reflect such a final pronouncement, with the exception of his blank, unavailing look. Most worrying, however, was his hand: it had changed colour and swollen to double its size. Blood seeped from the slit they had made, and dripped onto the ground, to Zachary's horror. Aproximado took charge of the situation and declared:

—*Let's take advantage of this to get him back to the city.*

Zachary hoisted Silvestre in his arms, although he was no weight to carry. He was just dozy, deprived of body. He was sweating like a fountain and, every so often, was shaken by violent tremors.

—*The man needs to be in hospital.*

Uncle's orders were precise and swift. We would all leave together, we'd get out of Jezoosalem before our father got his wits back.

—*Mwanito, go and get your things. Run.*

I entered my room, ready to rummage through every nook and cranny. But suddenly, I came to my senses: what did I have in the way of things? My only possessions were a pack of cards and a bundle of notes buried in the back garden. I decided to leave all these memories where they were. They were part of the place. The papers that I'd scribbled on were bits of me that I had stuffed into the soil. I had planted myself in words.

—*Ntunzi, aren't you going to take your case?*

—*I'm only taking the map. The rest, I'll leave here.*

Ntunzi went out. I couldn't resist glancing into his case. It was empty except for a cloth folder tied with string. I undid the strings and dozens of papers fell out. In each one, Ntunzi had drawn women's faces. There were dozens of faces, all of them different. In the corner of each piece of paper, he had written: "Portrait of my mother, Dordalma." I gathered the drawings together and put them back in the case. Then, I dashed out without even taking a last look around the room. When we are children, we never take our leave of places. We always think we'll be back. We never believe it's the last time.

I was the first to climb into the truck. Ntunzi sat next to me, at the back. Zachary appeared as we had never seen him before. For the first time, he was in civilian clothes. He was weighed down by a rucksack on his back.

—*Is that all you're taking, Zachary?*

—*I'll be back later. We're in a hurry now.*

Aproximado and Zachary went to fetch my old father. I still thought he might dig in his heels and refuse to come. But no. Silvestre came, walking like a child and as obediently as a servant. He installed himself in the front passenger seat, and made room for the Portuguese woman to sit beside him.

The truck lurched forward with a whine and then advanced slowly, passing the entrance gate and leaving in its wake a cloud of dust and fumes.

Seated on top of the baggage, Ntunzi was exultant, and he held my shoulders with both hands:

—*We're going to the city, little brother. I can't believe it . . .*

I turned my face away: before long my brother would be shedding tears of joy and at that moment all that I wanted were my impure feelings, in which happiness was mixed with nostalgia. I waved farewell, without realizing that there was no one on the other side. The only creature left in Jezoosalem was neither human nor alive: Jezebel, may God rest her soul.

—*Who are you saying goodbye to?*

I didn't answer. It wasn't Jezebel I was taking my leave of. I was saying farewell to myself. My childhood had been left on the other side. By setting out on this journey, I had ceased being a child. Mwanito had stayed behind in Jezoosalem, and I needed a new name, a new baptism.

That was when the vision struck me: without any other wind apart from the breeze produced by our old truck, the trees around us began to detach themselves from the ground and to flutter like ungainly green herons.

—*Look, brother! They're herons . . .*

Neither Ntunzi nor Zachary heard me. Then, it occurred to me that I should take a photo of these flying pieces of vegetation. Mine was a strange appetite: for the first time, it wasn't enough for me to see the world. Now, I wanted to see the way I looked at the world.

I got up and leaned on the roof of the passenger cabin to ask Marta for her camera. Standing there, I faced the road as if it were cutting me in half as it passed under the vehicle, separating joy from sadness.

When I managed to get a glimpse of the front seat, I got a surprise: my father and the Portuguese woman were hand in hand. The two of them were sharing a silent conversation about their respective nostalgias. I didn't have the courage to interrupt their silent dialogue. So I sat down again, a piece of baggage among all the other baggage, a relic among other dust-covered relics.

Two days passed with brief pauses and the continual roar of the vehicle's engine. At the end of the second day of the journey, as I slept with the swaying of the truck, I was no longer aware of the road. I was awoken with a start by Ntunzi's nudges. For the first time, we were going through a town. That was when I stared in wonder at streets crowded with people. Everything was exhilarating. The urban bustle, the cars, the advertisements, the street hawkers, the bicycles, kids like me. And the women: in pairs, in groups, in throngs. Full of clothes, full of colours, full of laughter. Wrapped in capulanas, concealing their mysteries. My mother, Dordalma: I saw her in every woman's body, every face, every burst of laughter.

—*Look at the people, Father.*

—*What people? I can't see anyone.*

—*Can't you see the houses, the cars, the people?*

—*Absolutely nothing. Didn't I tell you it was all dead, all empty?*

He was feigning blindness. Or had he really been blinded as a result of the snake bite? While Silvestre sat hunched in his seat, Marta held her cellphone out of the window, turning it this way and that.

—*What are you doing, Miss Marta?*— Zachary asked.

—*I'm seeing if I can pick up a network signal*— she replied.

She was obliged to bring her arm in. But for the remainder of the journey, Marta's arm swivelled this way and that like a rotating antenna. It was longing that guided her hand, seeking a signal from Portugal, a voice to comfort her, a word that would steal her back from geography.

—*So when do we arrive, Zaca?*

—*We already arrived some time ago.*

—*We've arrived in the city?*

—*This is the city.*

We had arrived without noticing where the rural world had ended. There was no clear border. Merely a transition in intensity, a chaos that got more dense: nothing more than that. In the passenger cabin, my father intoned, with a morbid shake of his head:

—*Everything's dead, everything's dead.*

There are those who die and are buried. That was the case with Jezebel. But cities die and decay before our noses, their entrails exposed, infecting us within. Cities decay within us. That's what Silvestre Vitalício said.

* * *

At the entrance to the hospital, our old father refused to get out of the truck.

—*Why do you want to kill me?*

—*What are you talking about, brother?*

—*It's a cemetery, I know perfectly well what it is.*

—No, Father. It's a hospital.

The family's efforts to get him out of the vehicle were all in vain. Aproximado sat down on the sidewalk, his head in his hands. It was Zachary who thought of a way to get us out of the impasse. If old Silvestre hadn't died, then his case was no longer as urgent as it had been in the beginning. We should go home. The neighbour, Esmeralda, who was a nurse, could then be called in to treat him in his own home.

—Let's go home, then!— Ntunzi agreed enthusiastically.

To me, it sounded strange. Everyone in our group was returning. Not me. The house where I was born had never been mine. The only home I'd ever had were the ruins of Jezoosalem. Next to me, Zachary seemed to hear my silent fears:

—You'll find you'll still remember the place where you were born.

As I contemplated the front of the house, it was obvious that nothing there meant anything to me. The same seemed to be happening to Silvestre Vitalício. Aproximado undid the various padlocks that secured the grilles on the doors. This operation took some time, during which my father stood there, his head bowed, like a prisoner in front of his future cell.

—It's open— Aproximado announced. —You go in first, Silvestre. I'm the one who lives here, I'm the one with the keys. But you're the owner of the house.

Without saying a word, and using only gestures, Silvestre made it clear that no one apart from himself and me would go through that door. I followed, protected by his shadow, stepping only on the dust on which he had trodden.

—First, the smells— he told me, filling his lungs.

He closed his eyes and sniffed at odours that, for me, did-n't exist. Silvestre was inhaling the house, kindling memories in his heart. He stood in the middle of the room, filling his chest.

—It's like a fruit. We first taste it with our nose.

Then he used his fingers. All he had was the hand that the snake had spared. It was the fingers of that hand that crawled over furniture, walls and windows. It was as if he were becoming familiar with his body again after a long period in a coma.

I confess: no matter how much I tried, I still found the house where I was born alien. No room, no object, brought back memories of the first three years of my life.

—Tell me, my son, I've died and this is my coffin, isn't it?

I helped him to lie down on the sofa. He asked for some silence and I let the house speak to him. Silvestre seemed to have fallen asleep when he stirred in order to take off the bandage round his hand.

—Look, son!— He called me, holding out his arm towards me.

The wound had disappeared. There was no swelling, no sign of anything. He asked me to take the bandage to the kitchen and burn it. I hadn't even found my way down the corridor when I heard his voice again:

—I don't want a nurse or any other stranger here in the house. Much less the neighbours.

For the first time, Silvestre was admitting the existence of others beyond our tiny constellation.

—The devil always dwells among the neighbours.

* * *

With the exception of Zachary, all of us lodged in our old house. Aproximado occupied the double room, where he already slept with Noci. Ntunzi shared a room with our father. I shared mine with Marta.

—It's only for a few days— Aproximado maintained.

A curtain separated the two beds, protecting our privacies.

184

When we arrived, Noci was still at work. At night, when she came into the house, Marta was lying there, apparently sleeping. Noci woke her up by stroking her hair. The two hugged each other tightly, and then wept inconsolably. When she was able to talk, the young woman said:

—*I lied, Marta.*

—*I already knew.*

—*You knew? Since when?*

—*Ever since the first time I saw you.*

—*He was ill, very ill. He didn't even want anyone to see him. In a sense it was good that I arrived late. If you'd seen him at the end, you wouldn't have recognized him.*

—*Where was he buried?*

—*Near here. In a cemetery near here.*

As the foreigner held Noci's hand, she turned a silver ring on the other woman's finger. Without even having to ask, Marta knew that the ring had been a gift from Marcelo.

—*Do you know something, Noci? It did me good to be there, at the reserve.*

The Portuguese woman explained: going to Jezoosalem was a way of being with Marcelo. The journey had been as reinvigorating as a deep sleep. By sharing in that pretence of a world coming to an end, she had learnt about death without grieving, departure without leave-taking.

—*You know, Noci. I saw women washing Marcelo's clothes.*

—*That's impossible . . .*

—*I know, but for me, those shirts were his . . .*

Any item of clothing drifting in a current of water would always be Marcelo's. The very substance of all the rivers in the world is surely made of memories resisting the flow of time. But the Portuguese woman's rivers were increasingly African ones: more sand than water, more the fury of nature than gentle, well-mannered watercourses.

—*Let's go together to the cemetery tomorrow.*

* * *

The following morning, I was left at home to look after my father. Silvestre got up late, and while still sitting in his bed, called for me. When I arrived, he sat there examining his own body. It had always been like that: my father forced one to wait before he started talking.

—*I'm worried about you, Mwanito.*

—*Why's that, Father?*

—*You were born with a big heart, my son. And with such a heart, you are incapable of hating. But for this world to be loved, it needs a lot of hatred as well.*

—*I'm sorry, Father, but I don't understand you at all.*

—*It doesn't matter. What I want you and I to agree to is this: if they want to take me into town, don't let me go, my son. Do you promise?*

—*I promise, Father.*

He explained: the snake hadn't just got his hand. It had bitten him all over his body. Everything around him was painful, the whole city enfeebled him, the wretchedness of the streets hurt him more than the contamination of his blood.

—*Have you seen how the most scandalous luxury lives cheek by jowl with misery?*

—*Yes*— I lied.

—*That's why I don't want to go out.*

Jezoosalem had allowed him to forget. The snake's poison had brought him time. The city had caused him to go blind.

—*Don't you feel like going out, like Ntunzi?*

—*No.*

—*Why not?*

—*There's no river here as there is there.*

—*Why don't you do like Ntunzi who's not here and is off buzzing around?*

186

—*I don't know how to walk . . . I don't know how to walk all over the place.*

—*My son, I feel so guilty. You're so old. You're as old as I am.*

I got up and went to the mirror. I was a young boy, my body still in first flush. Yet my father was right: tiredness weighed upon me. I had reached old age without deserving it. I was eleven years old, and I was withered, consumed by my father's delirium. Yes, my father was right. He who has never been a child doesn't need time in order to grow old.

—*One thing I hid from you, back there in Jezoosalem.*

—*You hid the whole world from me, Father.*

—*There was something I never told you.*

—*Father, let's forget about Jezoosalem, we're here now . . .*

—*One day, you'll go back there!*

—*To Jezoosalem?*

—*Yes, it's your homeland, your curse. Do you know something, son? That place is full of miracles.*

—*I never saw any.*

—*They're such tiny little miracles that we don't realize they've happened.*

* * *

We had been in the city for three days and Silvestre hadn't even opened the curtains. The house was his new refuge, his new Jezoosalem. I don't know how Marta and Noci managed to convince my father to go out that afternoon. The women thought it would do him good to see the grave of his late wife. I went with them, carrying flowers, at the rear of the cortège as it made its way to the cemetery.

As we lined up before my mother's tomb, Silvestre remained impassive, empty, oblivious to everything. We stared at the ground, he looked up at the birds streaking across the clouds. Marta handed him the wreath of flowers and asked him to place it on the grave. My father proved unable to hold the flowers, which fell to the ground, and the wreath broke apart. In the meantime, Uncle Aproximado joined us. He removed his hat and stood there respectfully, eyes closed.

—*I want to see the tree*— Silvestre said, breaking the silence.

—*Let's go*— replied Aproximado, —*I'll take you to see the tree.*

And we headed for the open ground next to our house. A solitary casuarina defied the sky. Silvestre fell to his knees before the old trunk. He called me over and pointed to the tree's canopy:

—*This tree, my son. This tree is Dordalma's soul.*

A BULLET BITTEN

To cross the world's desert with you
Face together death's terror
See the truth and lose fear
I walked beside your steps

For you I left my realm my secret
My swift night my silence
My round pearl and its orient
My mirror my life my image
I abandoned the gardens of paradise

Out here in the harsh day's light
Mirrorless I saw I was naked
And this wasteland was called time

With your gestures I was thus dressed
And learnt to live in the wind's full force

Sophia de Mello Breyner Andresen

We are daytime creatures, but it's the nights that give us the measure of our place. And nights only really fit comfortably in our childhood home. I had been born in the residence we now occupied, but this wasn't my home, it wasn't here that sleep descended upon me with tenderness. Everything in this dwelling made me feel a stranger. And yet, my slumber seems to have recognized something familiar in its tranquillity. Maybe that was why, one night, I had a dream that I'd never had before. For I fell into a deep abyss and was carried away by waters and floods. I dreamed that Jezoosalem was submerged. First, it rained on the sand. Then on the trees. Later, it rained on the rain itself. The camp was transformed into a riverbed, and not even continents were enough to absorb so much water.

My papers were released from their hiding place and ascended to the surface to ride along on the churning waters of the river. I went down to the shore to collect them. When I held them in my hands, something suddenly happened: the papers were turned into clothes. They were the sodden vestments of kings, queens and knaves. Each one of the monarchs passed by and handed over their heavy mantles. Then, devoid of their clothes, they floated on until they vanished in the calmer waters downstream.

Their clothes weighed so heavily in my arms that I decided to wring them out. But instead of water, letters dripped out of them and each one of these, upon hitting the surface, gave a pirouette and launched itself into the current. When the last letter had fallen, the clothes evaporated and vanished.

—*Marcelo!*

It was Marta who had just come ashore. She emerged as if from the mist and set off again in pursuit of the letters. She was shouting for Marcelo as her feet guided her with difficulty through the waters. And the Portuguese woman disappeared round the bend in the river.

When I got back to the house, old Silvestre asked about the Portuguese woman in a strangely anxious tone. I pointed back at the mist over the river. He got up in a rush, projecting himself beyond his own body, as if he were undergoing a second birth.

—*I'm on my way*— he exclaimed.

—*Where, Father?*

He didn't answer. I saw him stumble off in the direction of the valley and vanish among the thick bushes.

Some time passed and I almost fell asleep, lulled by the sweet song of the nightjars. Suddenly, I was startled by a rustling in the undergrowth. It was my father and the Portuguese woman approaching, supporting each other. The two of them were soaked. I ran out to help. Silvestre needed more help than the foreigner. He was breathing with difficulty, as if he were swallowing the sky in small doses. It was the Portuguese woman who spoke:

—*Your father saved me.*

I couldn't imagine how brave Silvestre Vitalício had been, nor how he had plunged into the swirling river, struggled against the current, and in the face of Death's designs had pulled her out of the waters where she was drowning.

—*I wanted to die in a river, in a river that rose in my homeland and flowed out into the end of the world.*

That's what the Portuguese woman said as she stared at the window.

—*Now leave me*— she added. —*Now I want to be alone with your father.*

I went out, smitten by a strange sadness. When I looked through the window, I seemed to see my mother leaning over her former husband, my mother returned from the skies and rivers where she had lingered her whole life. I knocked on the window and called, almost voiceless:

—*Mother!*

A woman's hand touched me, and before I could turn round, a bird perched on my shoulders. I slackened lethargically, and didn't offer any resistance when I felt myself being drawn upwards, my feet leaving the ground, the earth losing size, shrinking away like a deflating balloon.

* * *

I washed my face under the washtub tap as if only water could free me from my watery dream. Without drying myself, I looked out at the street through which the city flowed. Why was it that I had been dreaming about Marta ever since she had broken into the big house at Jezoosalem? The truth was this: the woman had invaded me just as the sun fills our homes. There was no way of avoiding or obstructing this flood, there was no curtain capable of blocking out such luminance.

Maybe there was another explanation. Maybe the Woman was already within me even before she arrived in Jezoosalem. Or perhaps Ntunzi was right when he warned me: water has nothing to learn from anyone. It's like women: they just know things. Inexplicable things. That's why we need to fear both creatures: woman and water. That, in the end, was the lesson of the dream.

* * *

After our outing to the cemetery, Silvestre Vitalício showed no further signs of life. He was an automaton, devoid of speech or spirit. We still believed it might be part of his recovery from the snakebite. But the nurse dismissed this explanation. Vitalício had sought exile within himself. Jezoosalem had isolated him from the world. The city had stolen him back from himself.

Aproximado said that the streets in our area were small and perfectly walkable. I should take my father to explore them, to see if he could be distracted. Now I know one thing: no street is small. They all hide never-ending stories, they all conceal countless secrets.

On one occasion, while we were walking along, I got the impression that my father was pushing me gently, guiding me. We passed by a Presbyterian church at the very time when they were holding a service. We could hear a choir and a tinkling piano. Silvestre stopped short, his eyes ablaze. He sat down on the steps leading to the entrance, his hands open across his chest.

—Leave me here, Mwanito.

He hadn't spoken for so long that his voice had become almost inaudible. And there, in that cold little corner, he remained for hours, stiff and silent. Even when the service had finished and the worshippers had left, Silvestre didn't move from the step. Some of the older ones greeted him as they passed by. The church and the street were dark and deserted when I pressed him:

—Father, please, let's go.

—I'm staying here.

—It's nighttime now, let's go home.

—I'm going to stay and live here.

I was familiar with my father's obstinacy. I returned home alone and alerted Ntunzi and Aproximado to old Silvestre's decision. It was Uncle who replied:

—Let's leave the fellow to sleep there tonight . . .

—Out in the open?

—He hasn't had so many houses for ages.

Early the next morning, I went into the street to find out what had happened to my father. When I found him, it was as if he hadn't changed his position, sheltering there on the steps where I had left him. I woke him with a gentle tap on the shoulder.

—Come on, Father. We'll come back tomorrow to listen to the hymns.

—Tomorrow? So when is tomorrow?

—In just a little while, Father. Come, I'll bring you back here.

So at the same hour every day for weeks and weeks, I took my father to the church steps, moments before the tuneful voices rose up to the heavens. Every time I tried to withdraw, he would grip me. Silently, and without moving so much as a finger, he wanted to share that instant with me. He was trying to re-create the veranda where we used to lay our silence to rest. Until, one day, I realized that he was murmuring the words of the hymns. Silvestre, even voiceless, was still joining in with the singers. Without anyone else being aware, Vitalício's words were ascending to the heavens. It was a lowly heaven, lacking in vitality. But it was the beginning of an infinity.

* * *

I awoke to the sound of female voices. I peered out of the window. Hundreds of people filled the street and were bringing the traffic to a halt. They were shouting slogans and brandishing placards on which one could read: *Stop the violence against women!* Among the throngs of people, I caught sight of Zachary Kalash, who was pushing his way towards our house. I opened the door and, without stopping to excuse himself, he pushed his way into the house as if he were seeking shelter.

—*What a racket these broads are making! Noci's there raising hell.*

He was wearing his military uniform and dragging a bag and a case along with him. I led him through to the kitchen which had, so to speak, been our room for entertaining visitors ever since our sudden, frenetic arrival.

—*Where's your brother?*— he asked me.

Ntunzi had come home less than an hour before, from yet another nightly escapade. He'd gone to bed still fully clothed, reeking of alcohol and cigarette smoke. Ever since his arrival in the city, my brother had hardly set foot in the house. From one night to the next, he hung out with people that Uncle Aproximado classified as "totally undesirable."

—*He's still sleeping.*

—Well, go and call him.

Zachary waited in the kitchen, but didn't sit down. He kept opening and closing the curtains as if the commotion in the street were disturbing him. "This world's finished!" I heard him complain. I stumbled about in the darkness of the room, shook Ntunzi and urged him to hurry. I went back to the kitchen and found the soldier helping himself to a beer:

—I'm going back to Jezoosalem. I've come to say goodbye.

Everyone had found a place for themselves. I'd rediscovered my childhood house. My father had found a home in madness. Only he, Zachary Kalash, hadn't found a place in the city.

—Are you going for good, Zaca?

—No. Only until I've completed certain duties.

—So what are you going to do in Jezoosalem?

—I'm not going to do anything, I'm going to undo . . .

—What do you mean?

—I'm going to blow up the ammunition store, and bury the weapons . . .

—You don't want any more wars, isn't that it, Zaca?

His face exhibited a sad, enigmatic smile. He seemed afraid of the answer. He ran his finger around the rim of the glass and produced a humming sound.

—D'you know something, Mwanito? I went to war to kill someone— and he waved his arm towards some vague presence.

—Someone?

—Someone inside me.

—And did you kill him?

—No.

—So what now?

—Now it's too late. That someone has already killed me.

When he was small, the same age as me, he wanted to be a fireman, to rescue people from burning houses. He'd ended

195

up setting fire to houses with people inside. A soldier of so many wars, a soldier without any cause at all. Defend the fatherland? But the fatherland he'd defended had never been his. That's what the soldier Kalash said, his words tumbling out as if he were in a hurry to finish his intimate revelations.

—*You know, Mwanito? Jezoosalem was more of a fatherland to me than any other. But anyway, let bygones be big ones . . .*

We were interrupted by the arrival of Ntunzi. Red eyed, his hair a mess, still unsteady on his feet from sleep. Zachary didn't even greet him. He opened his bag and pulled out a rucksack, which he tossed at the new arrival.

—*Take that rucksack to your room and pack your kit in it.*

—*Pack my kit? What for?*

—*You're going with me to Jezoosalem.*

—*Where?*— He fired back, laughing out loud, only to then proclaim in all seriousness:

—*Don't so much as think about it, Zachary, I'm not even leaving here dead.*

—*We'll only be a few days.*

I knew how arguments developed in our little tribe. Aware that tension would soon boil over into conflict, I intervened in an attempt to calm things down:

—Go on, Ntunzi. There's no problem in keeping Zachary company. It's just a question of going and coming back again.

—*He can go by himself.*

Zachary got up to face Ntunzi while at the same time drawing a pistol from a holster hanging from his belt. I stepped back, fearing the worst. But Kalash's voice had the calm of a will that has been mastered when he spoke:

—*Hold this pistol.*

My brother looked aghast, as startled as a newborn baby, with his limp hand barely able to sustain the weight of the gun. Kalash took a step back and contemplated Ntunzi's pathetic demeanour.

—*You don't understand, Ntunzi.*

—*What don't I understand?*

—*You're going to be a soldier. That's why I've come to fetch you.*

Ntunzi let himself collapse onto a chair, his eyes absorbed in nothingness. He sat like this for some time until Zaca Kalash took the pistol and helped him to his feet.

—*We already guessed what would happen to you here in the city. I'm not going to let you stay here any longer.*

—*I'm not going anywhere, you can't give me orders. I'm going to call my father.*

We followed my brother down the hall. The door to the bedroom was flung open, but Silvestre didn't bat an eyelid at the uproar. The soldier put an end to the argument with a yell.

—*I'm ordering you to come with me!*

—*The only one to give me orders here is my father.*

Suddenly, Silvestre raised his arm. Our old man wanted to speak. But all he could do was whisper:

—*Get out, all of you. You, Ntunzi, stay here.*

Zachary and I withdrew and sat down again at the kitchen table. Zachary opened another bottle of beer and drank, without another word. Outside, the cries of the demonstrators could be heard: "Women: protest, protest!"

—*Close the door so that your father can't hear it.*

When he came back to the kitchen, Ntunzi's spine was curved like a pregnant woman in reverse, such was the weight he seemed to bear, as he came over to me:

—*Goodbye, brother.*

I hugged him, but my arms were too short for so much bulk. My hands patted the canvas of his rucksack as if it were part of his body. Ntunzi and Zachary walked out of the door and I stood watching my brother recede as if the open road were to be his inescapable fate. They slowly pushed their way through the women demonstrators. As I got a better look at his way of walking, it seemed to me that in spite of his hang-over from the previous night, Ntunzi was marching forward with a military step, an exact copy of Zachary's.

I was drawing the curtains again when I noticed Noci waving at me. She was inviting me to go down and join the demonstration. I smiled, embarrassed, and closed the window.

* * *

Days passed during which all I did was be a father to my father. I looked after him, I took him places to which he invariably reacted like a blind man.

Until one day, I got a letter. I recognised Marta's hand-writing on the envelope. It was the first letter anyone had ever written to me.

THE IMMOVABLE TREE

Terror at loving you in such a fragile place as the world.

Woe at loving you in this imperfect place
Where everything leaves us broken and silent
Where everything deceives and divides us.

Sophia de Mello Breyner Andresen

I'm writing you this letter, dear Mwanito, so that we may take our leave of each other without saying goodbye. On the last day we were together, you told me about the dream you had had in which your father saved me from drowning in the river. If we take it that life is a river, then your dream was true. I was saved in Jezoosalem. Silvestre taught me how to find Marcelo alive in everything that is born.

I never tried to find out how Marcelo had died. For me, the explanation that he had died of an illness was enough. On the day I left, when I was already at the airport, Noci told me details of my husband's final journey. After Aproximado had left him by the gate, Marcelo must have wandered aimlessly for days, until he was shot down in an ambush. We can imagine where he went from the images that remained on his camera. Noci gave me these black and white photos. They were not, as I had supposed, pictures of water birds and landscapes. It was a report on his own end, an illustrated diary of his decline. From what we can glean, we can see that he wanted to escape from himself. At first by being dishevelled and shedding his clothes. Later, by behaving more and more like an animal, drinking water from puddles and eating raw flesh. When Marcelo was shot down, they took him for a wild animal. He wasn't killed in war. It was hunters. My man, dear Mwanito, chose this particular suicide. When death took him, he had already ceased to be a person. And in this way, perhaps he felt that he would die a lesser death.

It wasn't a continent that swallowed up Marcelo. He was consumed by his inner demons. Those demons went up in flames shortly before my return to Lisbon, when I burned all the photographs that Noci had given me.

* * *

Life only happens when we stop understanding it. Lately, my dear Mwanito, I have been far from understanding it. I never imagined myself travelling to Africa. Now, I don't know how I'm going to return to Europe. I want to go back to Lisbon, of course, but free from the memory of ever having lived. I don't want to recognize people or places or even the language that gives us access to others. That's why I got on so well in Jezoosalem: everything was strange to me, and I didn't have to account for who I was, or what course of life I should follow. In Jezoosalem, my spirit became light, free of any rigid structure, akin to the herons.

I have your father, Silvestre Vitalício, to thank for all this. I criticized him for having dragged you off to a wilderness. But the truth is that he established his own territory. Ntunzi would answer that Jezoosalem was founded on the deception of a sick man. It was a lie, of course. But if we've got to live a lie, let it be our own lie. Besides, old Silvestre didn't depart so far from the truth in his apocalyptic vision. For he was right: the world ends when we are no longer capable of loving it.

And madness isn't always an illness. Sometimes, it's an act of courage. Your father, dear Mwanito, had the courage that we lack. When all was lost, he began again. Even if, for the rest of us, it was meaningless.

That's the lesson I learnt in Jezoosalem: life wasn't made to be fleeting and of little consequence. And the world wasn't made to have boundaries.

* * *

When you began to read the labels on the weapons crates, it wasn't the letters that you learnt most. You were taught something else: words can be the curve that links Death and Life. That's why I'm writing to you. There is no death in this letter. But there is a farewell, which is a way of dying a little. Do you remember what Zachary used to say? "I've had all my deaths, fortunately, all of them were fleeting ones." My only death was Marcelo's. And that was certainly the first conclusive outcome. I don't know whether Marcelo was the love of my life. But it was a whole life's worth of love. Whoever loves, does so forever. Don't do anything forever. Except to love.

However, I'm not writing to you to talk about myself, but rather about your mother, Dordalma. I spoke to Aproximado, to Zachary, to Noci, to the neighbours. Every one of them told me bits of her life story. It's my duty to return this past that was stolen from you. People say that the story of someone's life is lessened in the account of their death. This is the story of the last days of Dordalma. Of how she lost her life after having been lost to life.

* * *

It was a Wednesday. That morning, Dordalma left home as she had never done before in her life: to be stared at and admired. She wore a dress to leave mere mortals groping and a neckline capable of making a blind man see heaven. She was so glorious that few noticed the little case that she was carrying with the same vulnerability as a child on its first day of school.

I'm beginning like this, Mwanito, because you have no idea how beautiful your mother was. It wasn't her face, or her waist, or her lithe, shapely legs. It was her entire being. At home, Dordalma was never more than gloomy, lifeless, and cold. Years of solitude and rejection had equipped her for nothingness, to be a mere native of silence. But on countless occasions, she would avenge herself in front of the mirror. There at the dressing table, she would garb herself in passing apparitions. She was, so to speak, like an ice cube in a glass. Disputing her place on the surface, reigning over this lofty abode until the time came for her to go back to being water.

So let me now go back to the beginning: on that Wednesday, your mother left home dressed to provoke fantasies. The looks she got from her neighbours were not appreciative of her beauty. There were sighs: of envy from the women; of desire from the men. The males gazed at her, their pupils dilated, their eyes predatory.

Here are the facts in all their bluntness and crudity. That morning, your mother climbed into the minibus and squeezed herself in between the men who filled the vehicle. The van set off amidst fumes, impelled by some strange sense of haste. The van didn't follow the usual route. The driver didn't pay attention to where he was going, distracted perhaps by the sight of his beautiful passenger in his rearview mirror. Eventually, the bus stopped in a stretch of dark, secluded wasteland. It pains me to write what happened next.

According to the few witnesses, the truth is that Dordalma was thrown onto the ground amid grunts and salivations, feral appetites and animal frenzy. And she sank further into the sand as if only the ground offered her fragile, trembling body protection. One by one, the men used her, shrieking as if avenging some age-old insult.

Twelve men later, your mother remained, almost lifeless, on the ground. During the hours that followed, she was no more than a corpse, a body at the mercy of ravens and rats, and worse than that, exposed to the mischievous looks of the few passers-by. No one helped her to get up. Countless times, she tried to recompose herself, but her strength failed her and she collapsed again, without a tear, her spirit gone.

Finally, after night had long fallen, your father appeared, creeping furtively like a cat among the rooftops. He looked around, took a deep breath and picked up his wife. With Dordalma in his arms, Silvestre crossed the road slowly, knowing that dozens of eyes were staring at his sinister figure from behind their windows.

He stopped abruptly by the front door, and stood there like a statue. In the pitch darkness it was impossible to see whether he was crying, whether his face was furrowed in resentment of the world and its hidden people.

He shut the door behind him with his foot and from then on, Vitalício's house was forever darkened. Silvestre placed your mother's body on the kitchen table and cushioned her head on bags and cloths. Then, he went to your room and kissed your brow and passed his hand over your brother's head. He turned the key in the lock and declared:

—*I'll be back in a minute.*

He returned to the kitchen to undress your mother. He left her naked, still unconscious, and made a bundle out of her useless clothes. He took the bundle out into the back garden and burnt the clothes after dousing them with gasoline.

He sat down again next to the table and watched over his sleeping wife. He made no gesture of affection or care. He merely waited, as aloof as a zealous functionary. As soon as the first signs of consciousness became visible on Dordalma's face, your father snapped at her:

—Can you hear me?

—Yes.

—Well, listen carefully to what I'm going to tell you: never shame me like this again. Do you hear?

Dordalma nodded, her eyes closed and he got up and turned away. Your mother placed her feet on the ground and sought her husband's arm for support. Silvestre dodged and blocked her way to the hall:

—Stay here. I don't want the children to see you in this state.

She was to remain in the kitchen, and get properly washed. Later, when the household was asleep, she could go to her room and stay there in peace and quiet. As for him, Silvestre Vitalício, he'd suffered enough vexations for one day.

* * *

Your father awoke, terrified, as if an inner voice were summoning him. His chest was heaving, his sweat flowing as if he were made solely of water. He went to the window, drew back the curtains and saw his wife hanging from the tree. There was a gap between her feet and the ground. He understood immediately: that tiny space was what separated life from death.

Before the street awoke, Silvestre, stepping swiftly, walked over to the casuarina, as if the only thing in front of him was some herbaceous creature made of leaves and branches. Your mother appeared to him like some dried fruit, the rope no more than a stem. He brushed aside the branches and silently cut the rope, only to hear the thud as the body fell to the ground. He regretted it immediately. He'd heard that sound before: it was the sound of earth falling on a coffin lid. That noise was to cling to his inner ear like moss on a sunless wall. Later on, your silence, Mwanito, was his defence against this recriminating echo.

For the second time in quick succession, Silvestre crossed the road with your mother in his arms. But this time, it was as if she had left her weight hanging from the gallows. He placed her body on the floor of the veranda and looked: there was no trace of blood, no sign of an illness or injury from a fight. If it weren't for the complete stillness of her breast, one would say she was alive. At this point, Silvestre burst into tears. Whoever passed that way would have thought that Silvestre had succumbed to the pain of death. But it wasn't his widower's state that was making him weep. Your father was crying because he felt scorned. A married woman's suicide is the worst indignity for any husband. Wasn't he the legitimate owner of her life? In that case, how could he accept such a humiliating act of disobedience? Dordalma hadn't abdicated from life: having lost possession of her own life, she had cast the spectacle of her own death in your father's face.

* * *

You already know what happened at the funeral. The wind deranged the graves, making it impossible to carry out a burial. Others were needed, the professional gravediggers, to complete the interment. Once home, after the funeral, Ntunzi was the most solitary of all the children in the world. No amount of affection from those present could console him. Only a word from old Silvestre Vitalício could heal him. But your father remained distant. It was you who passed through the crowd and took the widower's face in your little hands. Your hands offered Silvestre a refuge, tucked away inside a perfect silence. Maybe it was in that silence that he caught a glimpse of Jezoosalem, that place beyond all places.

After the funeral, your father shut himself away for days in the church. He didn't join in the choir, but he attended the service and later would lie around as if he were a beggar without a home to go to. Sometimes, he would sit down at the piano and his fingers would run up and down the keyboard dreamily. It was July, and the cold was such that one's hands, nestling in one's pockets, grow forgetful.

It was during one of these retreats that Zachary entered the church. He had just got back from the front line, and was still wearing a military coat. Kalash went up to your father and greeted him with a hearty hug. It looked as if they were hugging each other affectionately, but they were fighting. What they were whispering to each other sounded like words of consolation, but they were death threats. Whoever passed by would scarcely guess that they were in mortal confrontation. And no one could claim to have heard the shot. The blood dripping from Zachary's uniform as he left could never be taken as proof. Silvestre wiped the floor, and left no trace of the violence. There was no fight, no shot, no blood. To all appearances, the two friends had lingered in their embrace, comforting each other in their mutual grief at the disappearance of your dear mother, Dordalma.

* * *

Now you know why Ntunzi left with Kalash. Why he's destined to be a soldier, which has been the fate of generations in Zachary's family. Now you know why Silvestre feared the wind and the way the trees danced phantasmally. Now you know the purpose behind Jezoosalem and the exile of the Venturas away from the world. It wasn't just because your father was unhinged and that Jezoosalem was a chance product of his madness. For Silvestre, the past was an illness and memories a punishment. He wanted to live in oblivion. He wanted to lead his life far from guilt.

When you read this letter, I shall no longer be in your country. To be more precise, I shall be with Zachary: shorn of a country I can call my own, but sworn to serve causes invented by others. I'm returning to Portugal without Marcelo, I return without part of myself. Wherever I go I shall never find space enough for herons to soar in flight. In Jezoosalem, the earth will always contain more earth.

* * *

Noci once told me of the emptiness of her relationship with Aproximado. How their love had drained away over the course of time. Although our trajectories were so different, we both trod the same paths. I had left my home country to look for a man who was betraying me. She was betraying herself with someone who didn't love her.

—*Why do we put up with so much?*

—*Who?*

—*We women. Why do we put up with so much, with everything?*

—*Because we're afraid.*

Our greatest fear is loneliness. A woman cannot exist on her own, for she risks stopping being a woman. Either that or, for everyone's peace of mind, she becomes something else: a mad woman, an old hag, a witch. Or, as Silvestre would say, a whore. Anything but a woman. This is what I told Noci: in this world we are only somebody if we are a spouse. That's what I am now, even though I'm a widow. I'm a dead man's spouse.

* * *

I'm leaving you the photos we took, of our days in the game reserve. One of them, my favourite, shows the moonlight reflected in the lake. That night, I fear, was the last time I saw the moon. I still have some of its diffuse light left to illuminate the long nights that await me.

I want to thank you for everything that I experienced and learnt in this place of yours. The lesson I learnt is this: death separated me from Marcelo in the same way that we are parted from the birds by night. Just for a season of sadness.

We re-encounter our beloved on the next moonlit night. Even without a lake, even without night, even without the moon. They return to us ever more, within the light, their clothes floating in the river's flow.

I don't know whether I am happier than you: I have a house to go back to. I have my parents, I have my social circle in which I can live up to whatever expectations others have of me. Those who love me have accepted that I had to leave. But they insist that I return unchanged, recognizable, as if my journey were just a passing phase. You are a child, Mwanito. There is still a long journey, a lot of childhood, that you can live. No one can ask you to be only a keeper of silences.

You won't be writing back. I'm not leaving an address, or any sign of me. If you ever feel like finding out about me one day, ask Zachary. He gave me the task of regaining part of his past in Portugal. He wants his godmother back, he wants the magic of those letters to be reborn. One day, I'm sure, I'll come back to see you again. But there will never be another Jezoosalem.

THE BOOK

Never again
Will your face be pure clear and alive
Nor your stride like a fleeting wave
The steps of time weave.
Never again will I yield up my life to time.

Never more will I serve a master who may die.
The evening light shows me the wreckage
Of your being. Soon decay
Will swallow up your eyes and your bones
Taking in its hand your hand.

Never again will I love him who cannot live
For ever,
For I loved as if they were eternal
The glory, the light, the lustre of your being,
I loved you in truth and transparency
And am even bereaved of your absence,
Yours is a face of repulsion and denial
And I close my eyes so as not to see you.

Never more will I serve a master who may die.

Sophia de Mello Breyner Andresen

F ive years had passed since Marta, Ntunzi and Zachary had gone. One day, Aproximado called me to the room where Noci was, along with some kids from the neighbourhood. On the table, there was a cake with some candles stuck in the white sugar icing.

—*Count the candles*— my Uncle ordered.

—*What for?*

—*Count them.*

—*There are sixteen.*

—*That's how old you are*— Aproximado said. —*Today is your birthday.*

Never before had they given me a birthday party. In fact, it had never occurred to me that there had been a day on which I was born. But here, in this austere room in our house, the table was laid with cakes and drinks, decorated with streamers and balloons. On the icing of the cake, my name was written.

They went and got my old man, and sat him down next to me. One by one, the guests gave me their presents, which I piled clumsily on the chair by my side. All of a sudden, they started singing and clapped their hands. I realized that for a brief moment I was the centre of the universe. At Aproximado's instruction, I blew out the candles at one go. At that moment, my father stirred, and without anyone noticing, he squeezed my arm. It was his way of showing affection.

Hours later, after he had returned to his room, Silvestre retreated as usual into his shell. For five years, I was the one who looked after him, who guided him through the banalities of his daily routine, who helped him to eat and to wash himself. It was Uncle Aproximado who looked after me. He would often sit down in front of Silvestre, as one family member to another, and after holding his gaze for some time, would ask himself out loud:

—*Aren't you pretending to be mad just so as not to pay me what you owe?*

One couldn't detect so much as a hint of a reply on Vitalício's face. I appealed to Uncle's reason: how could play-acting be so convincing and long-lasting?

—*The thing is that they are old debts, left over from the days at Jezoosalem. Your father hadn't paid for his supplies for years.*

—*Not to mention the rest*— he added.

Aproximado never explained what this "rest" consisted of. And so his lamentations continued, always in the same tone: his brother-in-law never imagined how difficult it was to reach Jezoosalem by road. Nor how much a truck driver had to pay to avoid an ambush and escape attack. A secret of survival, he suggested, was to lunch with the devil and eat the leftovers with the angels. And he concluded, as if giving his intelligence a bit of spit and polish:

—*It serves me right. Business deals among relatives lead to . . .*

—*I can pay, Uncle.*

—*Pay what?*

—*What you're owed . . .*

—*Don't make me laugh, nephew.*

If there were debts, the truth is that Aproximado didn't take it out on me. On the contrary, he protected me like the son he never had. If it hadn't been for him, I would never have attended the local school. I'll never forget my first day in class, the strange feeling at seeing so many children sitting in the same room together. There was something stranger still: it was a book that united us for hours on end, weaving together childhood dreams in an aging world. For years I had taken myself to be the only child in the universe. And during that life, a solitary child was forbidden to look at a book. That was why, from the first lesson onwards, while the times tables and the alphabet flowed around the room, I caressed my notebooks and recalled my pack of cards.

My fascination for learning didn't go unnoticed by the teacher. He was a thin, wizened man, his eyes deep-set and grown old. He spoke passionately about injustice and against the newly rich. One afternoon, he took the group to visit the place where a journalist who had denounced corruption had been murdered. There was no monument nor any sign of official recognition in the place. There was just a tree, a cashew tree, to recall for posterity the courage of someone who had risked his life to expose dishonesty.

—Let us leave flowers on this sidewalk to clean away the blood; flowers to wash away the shame.

These were the teacher's words. With our master's money we bought flowers and we strewed them over the sidewalk. On our way back, the teacher was walking in front of me and I noticed how lacking in weight he was, so much so that I feared he might take off into the sky like some paper kite.

* * *

—Is that what he did?— Noci was astonished. —He took you to visit the people's journalist?

—And we left flowers, all . . .

—Well then, tomorrow you're going to take this teacher some papers. Plus a little letter I'm going to write . . .

I didn't know what was going through her head, but the girl didn't need any encouragement. At her command, I kept watch down the hall while she rummaged through Aproximado's drawers. She gathered together some documents, scribbled a short note and put everything in an envelope.

It was this envelope that I delivered to the teacher the following morning. By now, it was clear how ill our gentle master was. And he grew thinner and thinner until the merest clothing seemed too big on him. Eventually, he stopped coming and it wasn't long before we were told he had died. They later told us he had been suffering from the "sickness of the century."

That he had been the victim of the "pandemic." But they never mentioned the name of the illness.

Silvestre went with me to the teacher's funeral. In the cemetery, he passed Dordalma's grave. And he sat down with the weight of one who was never going to get up again. He remained there silent and unmoving, with only his feet brushing the sand, this way and that, like the continuous swing of a pendulum. I gave him a little time and then urged him:

—*Shall we go home, Father?*

There would be no going home. At that moment, I realized: Silvestre Vitalício had lost all contact with the world. Before, he almost never spoke. Now, he had stopped even seeing people. They were mere shadows. And he never spoke again. My old man was blind to himself. He didn't even have a home inside his own body.

That night, I thought about the deceased teacher. And I came to the conclusion that the "sickness of the century" was some sort of calcification of the past, an intermittent fever made of time. This illness ran in our family. The following day, I announced at school:

—*My father suffers from it too . . .*

—*What?*

—*The sickness of the century.*

They looked at me with pity and repulsion, as if I were the bearer of some perilous contagion. Friends avoided me, neighbours kept their distance. This exclusion by all, I have to admit, gave me a certain satisfaction, as if deep down I wanted to return to my solitude. And over time, I allowed myself to go astray. After the teacher's death, I lost interest in school. I would leave home in the morning, all dressed up for it, but I would stick around in the yard, scribbling down memories in the notebook I kept as a diary. When everything around had become darkness, my pages still preserved the light of day.

When I got home, I began to greet my father in the old way, in accordance with the rules of Jezoosalem:

—*I can go to bed now, Father. I've hugged the earth.*

Perhaps, deep down, I yearned for the immense hush of my sad past.

* * *

And then there was Noci, an additional reason for skipping school. Aproximado's girlfriend offered to help me with my homework. Even if I didn't have any, I invented it just to have her leaning over me, her huge dark eyes spearing mine. And then there was the bead of sweat running down between her breasts that I followed, doused and aroused by that drop, descending into her bosom until I sank into tremors and sighs.

Early in the morning, Noci would go around the house almost in a state of undress. I began to have erotic dreams. It wasn't new to me: female classmates, women teachers and neighbours had all made appearances in my daydreams. But this was the first time the gentle presence of a woman had placed the entire house under her spell. I found one thing out later: in the heat of the night, I wasn't the only one to have such dreams.

I don't know how much love Noci still gave to Aproximado. The truth is that we sometimes heard groans coming from their room. My father would toss and turn in his bed. He who had closed his ears to everything still had ears for this. On one occasion, I noticed that he was crying. It then became clear: Silvestre Vitalício would weep on the nights when the house was aglow with love.

Love is addictive even before it has happened. That's what I learnt, just as I learnt that dreams grow more intense the more they are repeated. The more I clamoured for Noci in my nightly ravings, the more real her presence became.

Until one night, I could have sworn that it was she, in the flesh, who furtively entered my room. Her figure slipped between my sheets and, during the moments that ensued, I sprawled across the intermittent frontier between our bodies. I don't know whether it was really she who visited me. I know that after she left, my father wept in the bed next to mine.

* * *

My uncle never tired of going on about how he hadn't been paid for his services to the family. But from what we could see, Silvestre's debts didn't leave Aproximado in any state of need. Our Uncle boasted of the money he made from the business of selling hunting permits. "But isn't that illegal?" Noci would ask. Well, what is illegal these days? One hand dirties the other and both imitate the gesture of Pontius Pilate, isn't that so? That's how Uncle responded. And not a day went by when he didn't return with fresh motives for rejoicing: he cancelled fines, turned a blind eye to infringements and conjured up complications for new investors.

—*Do you remember the truck I had during the war? Well nowadays, the apparatus of the State is my truck.*

One Sunday, his vanity led him to open out the map of the game reserve on the floor of the living room, and to summon me, my father and Noci:

—*See your Jezoosalem, my dear Silvestre? Well now, it's all private property, and I'm the one who's deprived of it, do you understand?*

My father's hollow look ranged over the floor, but failed to pause where his brother-in-law intended. Then suddenly Silvestre decided to get up and cross the room, dragging the map along with his feet so that it was ripped into large strips. Unable to contain herself, Noci laughed. Aproximado's breast unleashed a hitherto controlled anger:

—As for you, my dear, you're going to stay away from here.

—Is this your house?

—From now on, I'm the one who'll pay you visits in your house.

From then on, Noci appeared like the moon. Visible only at certain periods of the month. As for me, I became subject to the tides, periodically flooded by a woman.

* * *

Once, Noci turned up at the house mid-morning. She slipped furtively through the rooms. She asked after Aproximado.

—At this hour, Miss Noci?— I answered. *—At this hour, you know only too well, Uncle is at work.*

The girl went to the bathroom and, without closing the door, threw her clothes on the floor. I was suddenly smitten with a type of blindness and shook my head fearing I would never be able to see properly again. Then, I listened to the water from the shower, and imagined her wet body, caressed by her own hands.

—Are you there, Mwanito?

Embarrassment prevented me from answering. She guessed that I would be stuck in the doorway, incapable of peeping in, but without the strength to move away.

—Come in.

—What?

—I want you to find a box that's in my bag. I brought the box for you.

I went in bashfully. Noci was drying herself with the towel and I was able to catch glimpses of her breasts and her long legs. I pulled out a metal box and brandished it, trembling. She responded to my gesture.

—That's it. There's money inside. It's all yours.

Then she explained the origins of that little treasure trove. Noci belonged to a women's association that campaigned against domestic violence. Some months before, Silvestre interrupted one of their meetings and crossed the room in silence.

—*It was very strange what he did*— Noci recalled.

—*Don't take it too badly*— I rejoined. —*My father always had a negative attitude towards women, please forgive him . . .*

—*On the contrary. I . . . in fact all of us were very grateful.*

What had happened was this: Silvestre had crossed the room and had left a box with money in it on the table. It was his contribution to the campaign of those women.

In the meantime, the association had closed. A number of threats had sown fear among its members. What Noci was now doing was returning my father's gesture of solidarity.

—*Now, make sure you hide this cash from Aproximado, do you hear? This money's yours, yours alone.*

—*Only mine, Miss Noci?*

—*Yes. Like me, at this moment, I'm yours alone.*

Her towel fell to the floor. Once again, just like that first time in Jezoosalem, the presence of a woman took the ground away, and the two of us plunged into the abyss together. Afterwards, as we lay, exhausted on the tiled floor, our legs entangled, she passed her fingers over my face and murmured:

—*You're crying . . .*

I denied it fiercely. Noci seemed moved by my vulnerability and looking deep into my eyes, asked:

—*Who taught you to love women?*

I should have answered: it was lack of love. But no words occurred to me. Disarmed, I watched Noci buttoning up her dress, preparing to leave. When she got to the last button, she paused and said:

—*When he handed us the box of money, your father wasn't aware that among the notes, there was a bit of paper with instructions on it.*

—*Instructions? From whom?*

—*Your mother.*

My father had never realized this, but his deceased spouse had left a note explaining the origin and purpose for this money. It was Dordalma's savings and she was leaving this inheritance so that her sons should lack for nothing.

—*It was your mother. It was she who taught you how to love. Dordalma has always been here.*

And she placed the palm of her hand on my chest.

* * *

Then they came to get Uncle. An incrimination from an unknown source, we were told. Only I knew that the telltale documents had come from his drawer, and that it was his own girlfriend, with my complicity, who had sent the papers. When he came home, having paid his bail, Aproximado was suspicious of everything and of everyone. Above all, he suspected my father's secret powers. At dinner, taking advantage of Noci's absence, Aproximado spoke belligerently:

—*It was you, Silvestre, I bet it was you.*

My father didn't hear, didn't look, didn't speak. He existed in some other dimension and it was only his physical projection that appeared before us. Uncle resumed his menacing discourse:

—*Well let me tell you this: just as you arrived here, my dear Silvestre, so you'll be booted out. I'll have you exported like some hunting trophy.*

I could swear I detected a mocking smile on my father's face. It's possible his brother-in-law got the same impression because he asked in a tone of surprise:

—*What's happening? Has your hearing come back?*

Well, if that was the case, Silvestre had better listen. Whereupon Uncle launched forth with a litany of mishaps. My father got up from his chair abruptly and slowly poured the contents of his glass on the floor. We all understood: he was giving the dead something to drink, and was apologizing in advance for any ill omen.

—*It's too much, this is just too much!*— Aproximado roared.

The provocation meted out by his brother-in-law-widower had gone beyond all acceptable limits. Limping more than usual, Uncle went to the bedroom and brought back a photograph. He shook it in front of my nose and shouted:

—*Take a good look at this, nephew.*

His spirit suddenly and unexpectedly energized, my old man jumped onto the table and covered the photo with his body. Aproximado pushed him and the two fought for possession of the picture. I realized that it was my mother's image that was dancing around in Aproximado's hands, and I decided to join in the tussle. In no time at all, however, the paper was torn and each one of us ended up holding a piece in our fingers. Silvestre took hold of the remaining pieces and ripped them to shreds. I kept the portion I had ended up with. All it showed were Dordalma's hands. On her entwined fingers, could be seen an engagement ring. Once I was in bed, I kissed my mother's hands repeatedly. For the first time, I said goodnight to the person who had given me all my nights.

Before I fell asleep I sensed that Noci was coming into my room. This time she was real. Naked, she lay down next to me and I followed the contours of her body while losing the notion of my own substance.

—*You're the one who knows I'm here, you're the one touching me . . .*

—*Let's not make any noise, Miss Noci.*

—*This isn't noise, Mwanito. It's music.*

Music it may have been, but I was terrified at the thought of my father lying there next to us and, even more so, that Aproximado might hear us. But Noci's presence was more powerful than my fear. As she bounced up and down on my legs, I was afflicted once again by a doubt: what if women blinded me as they had my brother Ntunzi? I closed my eyes and didn't open them again until Noci shut the door as she left.

* * *

The following day, there was no day. Halfway though the morning, Aproximado was back from his office and his shouts reverberated down the hall.

—*Son-of-a-bitch!*

I shuddered: Uncle was insulting me after discovering that I, along with Noci, had betrayed him. The unequal echo of his steps approached down the hall and I sat on my bed expecting the worst. But his yells, when he reached the doorway, suggested something very different from my initial fears:

—*I've been punished! I've been transferred! You great son-of-a-bitch, I know it was you who fixed all this . . .*

The image of a once discreet and affable uncle vanished forever before our eyes. His gesticulations, as he stormed round old Silvestre's bed, were both grandiloquent and burlesque. He pulled out his cellphone as if he were drawing a pistol and declared:

—*I'm going to call your eldest son, he's the one who's going to take charge of this mess.*

And he went on moaning while he waited for his call to be answered. He'd had to put up with this nutcase all his life. Now he had this deadweight, in fact two deadweights, in his own home. He stopped his grumbling when he realized Ntunzi had answered. Aproximado told us he was going to turn the speaker on so that we could all hear the conversation.

—*Who's that? Is that Ntunzi?*

—*Ntunzi? No. This is Sergeant Ventura speaking.*

Can nostalgia sometimes take the form of a sudden lack of moisture in the mouth, a cold glow in the throat? In the stuffiness of that room, I swallowed drily upon hearing the evocative power of an absent voice. Aproximado repeated his acrimonious list of complaints against his brother-in-law. At the other end of the line, Ntunzi made light of it:

—*But old Silvestre is so feeble, so cut off from the world, so remote from it all . . .*

—*That's where you're wrong, Ntunzi. Silvestre is more heavy and troublesome than ever.*

—*My poor father, he's never been so harmless . . .*

—*Oh! Is that so? Well in that case tell me why he still calls me Aproximado? Eh? Why doesn't he call me Uncle Orlando, or even Uncle Godmother, like he always did before?*

—*Don't tell me you're thinking of kicking Silvestre out? Because it's his house.*

—*It was. I've already paid more than I should for it and for all the rest.*

—*Wait, Uncle . . .*

—*I'm the one giving the orders here, nephew. You're going to ask your regiment for some leave, and then you're going to come to the city and take these two useless creatures off my hands . . .*

—*And where do you want me to take them?*

—*To hell . . . or rather, to Jezoosalem, that's it, take them back to Jezoosalem again, who knows, maybe God's already there waiting?*

* * *

Straight after this, Aproximado packed up his things and left. Noci tried to organize a farewell dinner, but Uncle slipped out of it. What was there to celebrate? And off he went. Along with Aproximado went his girlfriend, my secret lover. In my desire, I got as far as invoking her, and in my dream, I made her recline on the empty double bed. But Noci showed no sign of herself. And I realized this: I had a body, but I lacked maturity. One day, I would go and look for her, and tell her how much I had remained faithful to her in my dreams.

* * *

One week later, Ntunzi returned home. He was elated, eager
for our reunion. He had progressed in his military career: the
stripes on his shoulders showed that he was no longer a common soldier. I had thought I would throw myself into my
brother's arms. But I surprised myself with my apathy and the
phlegmatic tone with which I greeted him:

—*Hi, Ntunzi.*

—*Forget Ntunzi. I'm Sergeant Olindo Ventura now.*

Shocked by my indifference, the sergeant stepped backwards and, frowning, showed his disappointment:

—*It's me, your brother. I'm here, Mwanito.*

—*So I see.*

—*And Father?*

—*He's in there, you can go in. He doesn't react . . .*

—*By the looks of it, he isn't the only one.*

The soldier turned on his heel and disappeared down the
hall. I listened to the inaudible murmur of his monologue in
my father's room. Shortly afterwards, he returned and handed
me a cloth bag:

—*I've brought you this.*

As I didn't move so much as a muscle, he himself took my
old pack of cards out of the bag. There were still some grains of
sand and a bit of dirt clinging to them. Faced with my impas-
siveness, Ntunzi placed the gift on my lap. The cards, however, didn't stay there. Without a hand to hold them, they fell
to the floor one by one.

—*What's wrong, little brother? Do you need something?*

—*I'd like to be bitten by the snake that attacked our father.*

Ntunzi stood there speechless, in a state of puzzlement.
He swallowed bitter doubts and then asked:

—*Are you all right, little brother?*

I nodded. I was as I'd always been. He was the one who

had changed. I was suddenly taken with the memory of how Ntunzi, when we were still in Jezoosalem, had announced his decision to abandon me. This time, his long, painful absence had had its effect and I had ceased feeling anything.

—*Why did you never visit us?*

—*I'm a soldier. I'm not in charge of my life.*

—*Not in charge? Then, why are you so happy?*

—*I don't know. Maybe because, for the first time, I'm in charge of others.*

From the interior of the house came sounds that were familiar to me. Silvestre was tapping the floor with his walking stick, calling me to help him go to the bathroom. Ntunzi followed me and watched me care for our old father.

—*Is he always like this?*

—*More than ever.*

We placed Silvestre back again in his eternal bed, without him even noticing Ntunzi's presence. I filled a glass with water and added a bit of sugar to it. I switched on the television, arranged the pillows behind his head and left him gazing vacantly at the luminous screen.

—*I find it strange: Silvestre isn't all that old. Is this death-like state of his for real?*

I didn't know what to answer. To be honest, is there any other way of living in this world of ours that doesn't involve deception?

* * *

Once back in the kitchen, an impulse made me throw myself at my brother. I hugged him at last. And our embrace seemed to last the duration of his absence. It only ended when his arm gently pushed me away. I was no longer a child, and I'd lost the ability to shed a tear. I took the pack of cards in my hands and shook the dust off it, while asking:

—*And what's the news of Kalash?*

Zachary Kalash was still hiding behind his soldier's disguise. But he was old, to be sure, much older than our father. One day, a military policeman stopped him to check where he'd got the uniform he was wearing. It was worse than false: it was a colonial uniform. Zachary was arrested.

—*Last week, he was freed.*

But he had other news: Marta was going to pay his fare to Portugal. Zachary Kalash was going to visit his wartime godmother, from the old days of military service.

—*It's a bit late now for him to see his godmother, don't you think?*

For sure, we fear death. But there's no greater fear than that which we feel at the idea of living life to the full, of living at full tilt. Zachary had lost his fear. And he was going to live. That's what Zachary had answered when my brother questioned him.

* * *

When we visited the cemetery, we stopped at Dordalma's grave. Ntunzi closed his eyes and said a prayer and I pretended to accompany him, ashamed that I'd never learnt any prayers. Afterwards, as we sat in the shade, Ntunzi pulled out a cigarette and was lost in his thoughts for a while. Something reminded me of the times when I used to help our old father fabricate silences.

—*So, Ntunzi, are you going to stay with us for a while?*

—*Yes, for a few days. Why do you ask?*

—*I'm worn out from looking after our father all by myself.*

It was lucky I didn't know how to pray. Because recently, I'd asked God to take our father up to Heaven. Ntunzi listened to my sad outburst, passed his hand down his leg and patted the top of his military boot. He took off his beret and put it back on his head again. I understood: he was preparing to make some solemn declaration. His soldier's status helped find the courage. He gazed at me lingeringly before he spoke:

—*Silvestre is our father, but you are his only son.*

—*What are you saying, Ntunzi?*

—*I'm Zachary's son.*

I pretended not to be surprised. I left the shade and strolled round my mother's tomb. And I mused over the countless secrets her gravestone concealed. So when Dordalma left home in the ill-fated van, it was Zachary she was going to meet. Now, everything made sense: the way Silvestre treated me differently. The guarded protection that Kalash always afforded Ntunzi. The anxiety with which the soldier carried my sick brother down to the river. Everything made sense. Even the new name Silvestre had given my brother. Ntunzi means "shadow." I was the light of his eyes. Ntunzi denied him the sun, reminding him of Dordalma's eternal sin.

—*Have you spoken to him, Ntunzi?*

—*To Silvestre? How could I when he shows no sign of life?*

—*I meant your new father, Zachary?*

No, he hadn't. They were both soldiers and there were matters that were not appropriate for conversation. For all misintents and purposes, Silvestre would remain his sole, legitimate father.

—*But look at what Zachary gave me. This is the last bullet, d'you remember?*

He showed it to me. It was the bullet lodged in his shoulder, the one he had never explained. It had been fired by my father during their scuffle at the funeral.

—*See? My father almost killed your father?*

—*There's just one thing I don't understand: why did they go off to Jezoosalem together?*

—*Guilt, Mwanito. It was the feeling of guilt that bound them . . .*

What Ntunzi then went on to tell me left me perplexed: the struggle between Zachary and Silvestre in the church didn't match what everyone thought. The truth was far removed from Marta's account. What, in fact, happened was this: overwhelmed by remorse, Zachary arrived late at the funeral, completely unaware of what had happened during the last hours of his beloved's existence. As far as he was concerned, Dordalma had committed suicide because of him. And that was why, burdened by the weight of his guilt, the soldier had turned up to express his condolences. In the church, Zachary had hugged my father, and like the good soldier that he was, declared his wish to restore his honour. Suffocated by his grief, he took out his pistol with the intention of putting an end to his own life. Silvestre clasped Kalash to himself in time to deflect the shot. The bullet lodged next to his collar bone. He would have shot himself through the heart if he hadn't been squeezed so hard, Kalash had lamented bitterly.

Later, as the soldier left the hospital where he had been treated, my old man avoided Zachary's attempt to give him a grateful hug:

—*Don't thank me. All I did was pay you back . . .*

* * *

My brother slept in the living room. That night, I couldn't get to sleep. I pulled up a canvas chair and sat down by the front door. It was misty and the dew made the surroundings hazy. I thought of Noci. And I missed the chasms she had opened beneath my feet. Maybe I would go and see her, if she persisted in staying away.

I half-expected to hear the door open. My brother couldn't sleep either. Holding the cards, he invited me:

—*Fancy a game, Mwanito?*

The game was just an excuse, of course. We played without talking, as if the result of the game were all-important. Then Ntunzi spoke:

—*On my way to the city, I passed by Jezoosalem.*

—*Aproximado said it's completely changed.*

It wasn't true. In spite of everything, time hadn't penetrated beyond the entrance to the game reserve. Ntunzi
assured me of this as he described in detail all that he had seen
of our old home. I stopped him before he began his account:

—*Wait a minute, let's bring father here.*

—*But won't he be sleeping?*

—*Sleeping is his way of living.*

We hauled old Silvestre out on our arms, and deposited
him so that he was reclining on the last step.

—*Now, you can go on. Tell us what you saw, Ntunzi.*

—*But can he hear anything? I think he can, isn't that so,
Silvestre Vitalício?*

In a loud voice, my brother embellished every detail, and
took me through his last visit. My father remained with his
eyes closed, unresponsive.

* * *

—*I spent a whole day in my past. One day in Jezoosalem.*

That's how Ntunzi began the account of his visit. He had
ferreted around for signs of our stay in the encampment,
looked for the secret notes that I had scribbled over the years
and buried in the garden. He visited the ruined buildings,
scratched the ground as if scraping his own skin, as if his memories were some lump hidden inside his body. And he rescued
the pack of cards from the hiding place where I had buried it.
That was the only testimony to our presence there.

He held the little pieces of card, and raised them up to the
sky as one does with the newly born. Some of them were faded
and illegible. Kings, knaves and queens had been dethroned
by the worms of time.

—*And after that, Ntunzi? What did you do, what happened
afterwards?*

My brother climbed up to look on top of the cupboard in our room and there was the old case where he had hidden his drawings. He shook the dust off them, so that he could see more clearly the dozens of sketches of our mother's face. All of them were different, but they all had the same large eyes of someone who is in the world as if standing at a window: waiting for another life.

* * *

Ntunzi interrupted his story, and suddenly knelt down to look into my father's face.

—*What's happened, Ntunzi?*— I asked.

—*It's Father . . . he's crying . . .*

—*No, he's always like that . . . it's tiredness, that's all.*

—*It looked to me as if he was crying.*

My brother had lost contact with us and no longer knew how to read our old father's face. I gathered up the cards and placed them in Ntunzi's hands.

—*Please, brother, read me the pack, remind me what I wrote.*

There followed moments as thick as a river in full flow. My brother pretended to be deciphering tiny letters among the beards of kings and the tunics of queens. I knew he was inventing almost everything, but for years, neither of us had been able to distinguish the frontier between memory and lying. Sitting in his chair on the veranda and swaying his body as my old father used to do, Ntunzi interrupted his reading when he saw that I was completely still.

—*Have you fallen asleep, Mwanito?*

—*Do you remember how I was cold and distant yesterday, when we met?*

—*I admit that I was taken aback. I'd chosen my smartest uniform . . .*

—*The problem is that I suffer from the same illness as our father.*

For the first time I confessed that which had been stifling my heart for ages: I had inherited my father's madness. For long periods of time, I was assailed by selective blindness. My inner being was invaded by the desert, which turned our neighbourhood into a community peopled by absences.

—*I have fits of blindness, Ntunzi. I suffer from Silvestre's sickness.*

I went to the drawer in the kitchen and pulled out my school folder, which I opened out before my brother's astonished look.

—*Look at these papers*— I said, holding out a bundle of pages covered in handwriting.

I had written all this during my moments of darkness. Assaulted by fits of blindness, I ceased seeing the world. All I could see were letters, everything else was shadows.

—*You are a shadow now.*

—*I've got a name that means shadow.*

—*Can you read the handwriting?*

—*Of course, this is your handwriting. Careful and neat, like it always was . . . Wait a minute, are you saying you wrote all this without seeing?*

—*My blindness lifts only when I write.*

Ntunzi chose a page at random and read out loud: "*These are my last utterances, Silvestre Vitalício proclaimed. Pay attention, my sons, because no one will ever listen to my voice again. I myself am taking leave of my voice. I say this to you: you committed a grave mistake in bringing me to the city. I am in the process of dying because of that perfidious journey. The frontier between Jezoosalem and the city wasn't based on distance. Fear and guilt were the only frontier. No government in the world is more oppressive than fear and guilt. Fear made me live, humble and withdrawn. Guilt caused me to flee myself, empty of memories. This is what Jezoosalem was: it wasn't a place but a time of waiting for a God to be born. Only such a God would alleviate the punishment that I had imposed on myself. Yes, only now do I understand: my sons, my two sons, only they can bring me that sense of forgiveness."*

His voice faltered and he stopped reading. My brother crouched next to Silvestre and read the last sentence again *". . . my sons, my two sons . . ."*

—*Did you say that, Silvestre?*

Faced with my father's passivity, Ntunzi turned to me and asked, his voice trembling with emotion:

—*Is this true, brother? Did Father say this?*

—*These pages contain all that is our life. And when is living, Ntunzi, for real?*

I tidied the sheets and put them away in the folder. And I gave him my book as my final and only belonging.

—*Here is Jezoosalem.*

Ntunzi clutched the folder and went back into the house. I watched my brother disappear into the darkness, while the memories returned of a time when we would erase our tracks to protect our solitary refuge. And I recalled the half-light where I had deciphered my first letters. And I remembered the twinkling light of the stars over the river. And striking off the days on the blackened wall of time.

Suddenly, I felt an immense longing for Noci. Maybe I'll go and look for her sooner than I thought. That woman's tenderness was confirmation for me that my father was wrong: the world hadn't died. In fact, the world hadn't even been born. Who knows, I may learn, in the attuned silence of Noci's arms, to find my mother walking across an endless wasteland before reaching the last tree.